William Peterfield Trent

The Authority of Criticism and Other Essays

William Peterfield Trent

The Authority of Criticism and Other Essays

ISBN/EAN: 9783337279585

Printed in Europe, USA, Canada, Australia, Japan

Cover: Foto ©Andreas Hilbeck / pixelio.de

More available books at **www.hansebooks.com**

THE AUTHORITY

OF

CRITICISM

AND OTHER ESSAYS

BY

WILLIAM P. TRENT

AUTHOR OF

"WILLIAM GILMORE SIMMS," "JOHN MILTON," ETC.

NEW YORK
CHARLES SCRIBNER'S SONS
1899

University Press:

JOHN WILSON AND SON, CAMBRIDGE, U.S.A.

TO

S. S. P. PATTESON, Esq.

Of the Richmond (Va.) Bar,

AS A TOKEN OF FRIENDSHIP.

PREFATORY NOTE

ALTHOUGH the papers contained in this volume were written from time to time and for special purposes, they will, I trust, be found to possess in the main a unity sufficient to warrant the reader in regarding them as something more than a mere collection of detached essays. I am not presumptuous enough to claim that in them I have outlined a critical philosophy, and given certain applications of it; but I think I may fairly say that I have endeavored to discuss some important critical and literary problems which must be satisfactorily dealt with before an adequate critical philosophy can be developed.

I suppose that few people will be rash enough to assert that such a philosophy exists already, and I hope that many will agree that unless it is developed in the future critics are likely to continue their uncomfortable and undignified floundering in the bogs of dogmatism and impressionism. Acting on these suppositions, I have ventured to investigate as well as I could such important topics — fundamental as they plainly are to a critical philosophy — as The Sanction and Scope of the Authority of Criticism; The Nature of Literature, with particular regard to its emotional basis; The Relations of Literature to Morals; and The Best Methods of Teaching Literature in the Schools.

To these mainly theoretical but in part practical papers I have added a few others, not merely to lend variety to the volume, but more particularly to illustrate in a somewhat concrete way the truth of principles contended for in the group of essays just specified. For example, the papers on Tennyson and Musset and on the Byron Revival will be found to bear upon the important topic of the emotional basis of literature. They were written, however, with no intention to prove a thesis, but simply as critical studies.

In conclusion, I must assure my reader that I arrogate to myself no discoveries, and that I am aware that I am probably as far from having an adequate critical philosophy

PREFATORY NOTE

as he is.   All I can positively affirm is that there is need of such a philosophy, and that honest groping for one on the part of men who have a high appreciation of the critic's function is perhaps the best means of attaining it.

W. P. TRENT.

The University of the South,
  Sewanee, Tenn., June 7, 1899.

*** Thanks are hereby returned to the editors of *The Forum*, *The Atlantic Monthly*, and *The Bookman*, for permission to reprint the first and sixth, the seventh, and the ninth essays respectively.

G.

CONTENTS

I

THE AUTHORITY OF CRITICISM

I

THE AUTHORITY OF CRITICISM

I

THE comparatively recent visit of M. Ferdinand Brunetière to this country has stimulated among us fresh interest in a question that is almost as old as the hills, and as varied in the forms it assumes; to wit, What is the weight of authority carried by criticism? Is there such a thing, men are asking themselves, as a science of criticism, or is all criticism at bottom merely the expression of an individual opinion, unsupported, or supported in varying degrees, by other individual opinions? If it is well-nigh impossible to eliminate the personal equation in strictly scientific experiments, is it worth while, they ask, to try to eliminate it from our studies in the semi-sciences, such as ethics and history, or in the arts? In other words, is not criticism a present, individual act; ought not the critic to say " I " instead of " we "; and is not every one of us that reads a book or looks at a picture as much master of his own likes and dislikes as the typical Englishman is lord of his own castle?

It is plain that this question is almost as old as the race; for it is fundamentally the question men have been asking themselves since primitive times, since the very first attempt on the part of some bold innovator to break up what the late Mr. Bagehot aptly called " the cake of custom." A conscious, or semi-conscious, assertion of the right of individual judgment is the basis of every step of progress that humanity has made; and, speaking loosely, the history of civilization is the history of the emancipation of the individual will and judgment. The authority of society has not indeed been abrogated; but it retains the force of law over our actions only, and principally on utilitarian grounds. " Society thinks so; therefore a thing is right " is a dictum that will stand in the way of few liberal-minded men in this year of grace.

But, if men have been daring to tell society for centuries that it is in error with regard to this or that point of ethics or politics, it is not surprising that they should long ago have mustered up courage to tell the small cultivated portion of society not only that it is in error with regard to particular books and objects of art, but that it is in error in thinking that it has any special call or right to pronounce judgment in such matters. This is precisely what Perrault did in his famous controversy with Boileau over the comparative merits of the ancients and the moderns.

About two centuries have elapsed since Perrault finished the third part of his " Parallèle "; and the controversy, with a somewhat shifted base, is still raging in France, with MM. Brunetière and Lemaître as protagonists. It is no longer a question of Homer and Virgil *versus* Chapelain, or even whether in translation Pindar is intelligible to the wife of a worthy French magistrate; but it is pretty largely a question of the importance of the seventeenth century, as compared with the nineteenth, and of the benefit to the student of classifying properly a work of art, compared with the benefit to be derived from treating such a work as an object of æsthetic or psychologic interest merely. In other words, the chief critical problem which the French mind is endeavoring to solve to-day is a more complex form of the problem with which it was struggling two centuries ago, and contains precisely the same elements that all great mental problems involve, viz., the value or worthlessness of what the present has preserved from the past, and the rights of the individual, as opposed to the claims of society.

Yet the controversy between the ancients and the moderns was not confined to France ; indeed, that country, as M. Brunetière shows, took up the question in a curiously belated fashion. And in like manner the present controversy between collective and individualistic, or, if we prefer, academic and impressionist, criticism, is not confined to the partisans of MM. Brunetière and Lemaître. In England the late Matthew Arnold did doughty battle for the cause of ordered criticism ; and Professor Saintsbury has for years been doing his best to wave the flag of the impressionists. In America Lowell's influence was, on the whole, conservative ; while Mr. Hamlin Garland, able and sincere writer though he be, and most of the strenuous admirers of Walt Whitman have borne the standard of individualism to a quite impregnable position — whether on the heights of reason or among the fens of folly must be determined later.

But, over and above the labors of individual critics, there are two forces at work in all parts of the Western world that continue to carry on this conflict, often unconsciously. These two forces are the teachers and the reporters. Nearly all persons who engage in any form of teaching are interested in preserving the sway of authority, and may be counted on the side of conservative criticism. On the other hand, men whose business it is primarily to amuse and interest, and only secondarily to instruct, society, are not led to uphold the sway of authority (save in matters of religion and politics about which their patrons may be sensitive) simply because what holds by the past is not likely to prove so interesting as what touches the present or looks to the future.

Reporters, then, — and the term practically includes all writers who minister to public curiosity, — may be counted, n most cases, on the side of individualistic criticism. That is to say, the reportorial spirit may be counted; for newspaper critics *per se* are usually hidebound sticklers for academic methods. As the reporter, owing to the waning force of traditional checks upon a mixed and rapidly evolving society, plays quite a part among us, and is likely to gain power rather than lose it in the near future, it follows that impressionist criticism will not lose ground in America for some time to come, even if it does not grow rampant. On the other hand, as our teachers and journalistic critics are rarely possessed of broad culture, the real force and value of the academic principles they stand for tend to become enfeebled and obscured. Hence, it is not so much a battle, of the critics that we are likely to observe in America, as a *mêlée*.

If all this be true, it would seem to be worth our while to endeavor to determine where the truth lies with regard to this vexed problem of the authority of criticism. If M. Brunetière is right, and M. Lemaître wrong, it will be well to try to check our present propulsion toward impressionism. If M. Brunetière is wrong, — I use his name only because he is plainly the foremost living representative of academic criticism, — then we may feel easy about the go-as-you-please methods of some of our critics, and may give ourselves up to quite a hedonistic cult of frank individualism. If, however, both of these distinguished men are right in part, and both are wrong in part, it is obvious that it all the more behooves us to seek to establish the proper limits of the principles of criticism each strives to apply; for the more complex our principles of thought and action, the more chance there is of our going dangerously astray in their

application. It is hardly necessary to add
that a presumption lies in favor of the last
hypothesis, not only because extremes are
rarely safe, but because two great critics, or
two numerous factions of critics, are not
likely to be enthusiastic supporters of oppos-
ing principles without having positive reasons
of weight to actuate and sustain them in their
contentions.

II

OUR first question is, then, whether M. Brunetière is right when he asks us to distrust our
individual judgment about a piece of literature, and to make a study of criticism and
literary history in order to discover the
proper value and rank of the work to be
judged, before we venture to form or express
a settled opinion concerning it. This is
practically what he does ask, although he
lays most stress on a particular demand; to
wit, that we shall pay special attention to the
matter of genres — that is, to the different
forms or categories of literature. It is also
what Matthew Arnold asked, although he laid
most stress on the matter of general culture.
But M. Lemaître demurs at once. He says,
in substance: You are leaving out of sight

the main object for which men write and read books, viz., to receive pleasure and, partly, to give it. Your abstract genres, your epics and dramas, creatures of your own brains, become your tyrants and doom you to hopeless drudgery. It is no longer possible for you to take up a book and simply enjoy it. I, too, could do your kind of criticism if I had a mind to; but if I did, I should be turned into a solemn magistrate, thinking forever of the black cap I must soon put on. — Now this demurrer has plainly its basis in common sense, and is a wholesome corrective of the claims of the academic critic when these take an extreme form. It is obvious that certain minds will always rebel at a hard and fast code of rules for critical reading, and that most minds will rebel sometimes. Not only are there books that we want to read without analysis, but there are times when we prefer simply to read a book that at other times we should be glad to analyze. We do not care to analyze The Prisoner of Zenda: it would scarcely pay us to analyze it, although one enterprising student of architecture has drawn an elaborate plan of the remarkable castle. Yet we were all eager to read it; and we are most of us glad now that we did read it. On the other hand, we ought at one time or another to make a careful analytic study of Shakspere's Sonnets; yet there are some of us who like to have a pocket edition of these divine poems with us on a railway journey, when careful study is plainly out of the question.

Again, we are constantly repeating to young people the injunction that they should begin to read classical poems and novels as soon as they are able to comprehend them; but we do not say at the same time that they must wait until they understand the main facts about the " evolution of genres " before they form an opinion of the general value and interest to themselves of the literature with which they have been brought in contact. In this case, however, we do apply a part at least, of M. Brunetière's critical philosophy; for we rely chiefly on the verdicts of past generations in our choice of the classics we recommend to the young. Still, it remains true that the most critically minded of us cannot be critical always, and that large classes of readers can never be critical in any true sense of the word. So M. Brunetière's principles hold good for only a small body of readers, and not at all times and seasons even for these. It is idle, however, to think that he has ever meant them to be taken strictly by the majority, by what we call politely the reading public; yet there is a sense in which they may be laid to heart by every one, and inculcated even in a very young child.

III

REDUCED to their lowest terms, the principles for which most academic critics stand are, I think, three in number: (1) That due weight should be given to the collective wisdom of the past and the trained knowledge of the present; (2) that there are more or less ascertainable degrees of value in the various genres of artistic production; and (3) that no art can be absolutely divorced from ethics.

It follows at once from the assumption of these three principles that if it can be shown that a special kind of poetry, say the epic, is of greater value (that is, makes a higher and wider appeal to the minds and hearts of men in general) than another kind, say the elegy, it is not merely a mistake of judgment to prefer the latter to the former, but also, where sufficient knowledge is available,—a point which is covered by the first principle given above,— an ethical lapse of a more or less venial character. In fine, if there were such a person as a purely academic critic of perfect fearlessness, he would affirm that to prefer Gray's Elegy to Paradise Lost is not only foolish, but wrong: for this is the sense in which he accepts the dictum that art cannot be divorced from ethics; it being quite possible for an academic critic to acquiesce in the truth of the maxim " Art for art's sake," provided it be interpreted rationally. In other words the academic critic, while he may not judge works of art from a preconceived ethical point of view, and demand that they serve some definite ethical purpose, will, if he be consistent, assert emphatically that, as no judgment can be formed without entailing some corresponding responsibility, and as objects of art must be judged before we can determine whether the emotions produced by them are really wholesome or harmful, it follows that art, by entailing responsibilities upon all who are brought into contact with it, — and what experience in life does not entail upon us the responsibility of determining whether it be wholesome or harmful? — cannot in the last analysis be divorced from ethics.

If, now, it be urged that what we ought to examine and pass judgment upon is not the object of art that produces emotions in us, but ourselves who experience these emotions, the critic will reply that he has always maintained the necessity for self-examination in æsthetic matters, but that, if a doubt be implied with regard to the possibility of obtaining valid objective judgments in the domain of the arts, such doubt must apply as well to the ultimate validity of all other objective judgments, with the result that we are landed either in pure idealism or in universal scepticism. An objection, however, that is so far-reaching is practically no objection at all.

But certainly this strange doctrine, that it is in some way wrong to prefer a poem, a picture, or a statue of an inferior genre to one of a superior genre, will not be admitted by many persons without considerable protest. Yet, if it be once granted that there are higher and lower forms of art, and that it is the duty of every man, not merely to act on the highest level possible, but also to expose his soul to the highest influences possible, it follows that to prefer wilfully the lower to the higher in any particular is, strictly speaking, an ethical lapse. Many of us are, of course, absolved from all blame in this regard on account of our ignorance in the premises: those of us who are not ignorant have generally tried to justify ourselves by affirming that, while there may be genres, there is no proof that one is higher than another; that it is a mere assumption of *a priori* criticism to say, for example, that a fine ode like Gray's Progress of Poesy is *per se* superior to the same poet's Elegy Written in a Country Churchyard, — an opinion held, perhaps, both by Gray himself and by Matthew Arnold.

The answer made by the academic critic to this contention will naturally bring into question his first principle, viz., that due weight should be given to the collective wisdom of the past and to the trained knowledge of the present. The ode, he will say, stands at the head of all forms of lyrical poetry, because in it the subjective emotions of the poet are fused to a white heat. The ancients regarded the ode as the greatest of lyrical forms; and modern students of poetry have as yet seen no reason to abandon this view. The finest ode of Pindar ought then to be superior to any elegy of Mimnermus, and Gray's ode should outrank his Elegy, unless in the former poem the poet has fallen below the level proper to the genre selected, and in the latter poem has risen to an equal or greater degree, — a phenomenon which seems to have occurred, if the two pieces be regarded as wholes, and which both explains and justifies the popular verdict in the matter.

This answer shows us at once how interdependent the three principles of the academic critic really are. If there are genres of higher and lower value, then it is our duty to try to put ourselves in greater sympathy with the higher than with the lower; or, in other words, we cannot, if we would, divorce art from ethics. But we cannot establish our contention that there are superior and inferior genres, unless we insist that due weight be given to that collective wisdom of the past which has established and differentiated the various genres. It is the conscious, or unconscious, perception of the interdependence of these principles of academic criticism that has led the impressionists, who generally desire to escape from ethical responsibility, to attack with relentless vigor that deference to the judgment of the past inculcated by the first principle. They cannot well attack the second part of this principle, that due weight should be given to the trained knowledge of the present; for this would be to undermine the authority of their own privileged order of *mandarins:* they

can, however, say much about a servile
dependence on an effete past.

But, if the collective wisdom of the ages
be of paramount importance in ethics, philosophy, law, and all studies in which fresh
material for experimentation is not being
continually introduced, it is difficult to see
how its authority, within reasonable limits,
can be questioned with regard to criticism.
That genres exist even in art is a fact as well
determined as the existence of the various
mental faculties. That we do not know the
ultimate nature of art in the one case, or of
mind in the other, does not prove that we
have no need of the hypotheses of criticism
and of metaphysics. That there is a hierarchy of genres is a fact as well proved as
that there is a hierarchy of mental powers
or of bodily functions.[1] To cut the Æneid

---

[1] With regard to this important matter of the hierarchy
of the genres one cannot do better than to follow Brunetière in quoting Taine : " Dans le monde imaginaire, comme
dans le monde réel, il y a des rangs divers parce qu'il y
a des valeurs diverses. Le public et les connaisseurs as-
signent les uns et estiment les autres. Nous n'avons pas
fait autre chose depuis cinq ans, en parcourant les écoles
de l'Italie, des Pays-Bas, et de la Grèce. Nous avons
toujours, et à chaque pas, porté des jugements. Sans le
savoir nous avions en main un instrument de mesure.
Les autres hommes sont comme nous, et en critique comme
ailleurs il y a des vérités acquises. Chacun reconnaît

out of Latin literature would be like putting out a man's eye: to cut out Juvenal's Satires would be like amputating a finger. "Solvitur inquirendo." Ask even the most rampant impressionist — except, perhaps, the ultra-Whitmanite — which he would rather have written, Shakspere's dramas or Burns's songs, Scott's romances or Maupassant's tales, Gibbon's Decline and Fall or Macaulay's Essays, and the answer will nearly always indicate a tacit acceptance of the theory of a hierarchy of genres. "A mere instance of the force of convention," the Whitmanite might say, "Walt Whitman's Leaves of Grass put all the genres to the blush, and the academic critics, too. You will not dare to mention Shakspere and Milton in the same breath with him!" An advocate of free love might make just such a reply to an argument in favor of monogamy.

In fact it can be easily shown that the distinctions and gradations sanctioned by the

aujourd'hui que certains poètes, comme Dante et Shakspere, certains compositeurs, comme Mozart et Beethoven, tiennent la première place dans leur art. On l'accorde à Goethe, parmi les écrivains de notre siècle; parmi les Hollandais, à Rembrandt; parmi les Vénitiens, à Titien. Trois artistes de la Renaissance italienne, Léonard de Vinci, Michel-Ange, et Raphaël, montent d'un consentement unanime au-dessus de tous les autres." [L'Évolution des Genres, I. (De la Critique), p. 273.]

great critics of the past, and upheld by the arguments of the academic critics of the present, are founded on just the same basis as the distinctions and gradations established and supported by the jurist and the scientific moralist. The critic may often deal with matters of less transcendent importance than his fellow-students: but his science, in the last analysis, is as securely based as theirs; for all three ultimately rest on authority and present judgment. He has no such sanctions to rely upon as the jurist and the moralist have; hence he is often doomed to see un-informed opinions prevail:[1] his domain is one that can be easily entered from all sides; hence he is compelled to struggle with nu-merous rivals who are continually betraying the cause of the science he serves. But he feels that his position is at bottom as secure as that of any student of any semi-science can be; and he bides his time in the hope of better days.

[1] "But anybody is qualified, according to everybody, for giving opinions upon poetry. It is not so in chymis-try and mathematics. Nor is it so, I believe, in whist and the polka. But then these are more serious things." [Elizabeth Barrett to Robert Browning, Feb. 17, 1845.]

IV

WE have now seen what, in brief, are the contentions of the academic critic; and we must admit that if his claim, that criticism rests for its authority on the same basis as ethics and law, be established, it is expedient for us, if not incumbent upon us, to give criticism its due influence in the formation of our literary and artistic tastes and judgments. Could we once bring ourselves to do this, we should find that the parallel between criticism and its sister semi-sciences holds very closely. Just as there are some ethical principles acted upon by all civilized men, others acted upon chiefly by certain races, others only by individuals of a high type of character, so there are principles of criticism universal, racial, and individual in their application. For example, all men have practically agreed — at least till the present generation — to regard poetry as superior, on the whole, to prose; the French have practically agreed that the drama which preserves the unities is the best for their stage; most highly cultured individuals are agreed in giving a greater value to the sonnet as a poetic form than would be accorded it by the average reader. In the light of these facts we must infer that there are some principles of criticism so binding upon us that we ought to endeavor not only to make an individual application of them, but also to inculcate them in our children; others which, as Americans, Englishmen, Frenchmen, or what not, it will probably be to our advantage to follow; still others which, in all likelihood, will appeal to us more and more as we advance in culture. In short, no man who is seeking to develop his literary and artistic taste and judgment can afford to be a thoroughgoing impressionist any more than he can afford to be an absolute individualist in his daily life and conduct.

If there be any force in the above reasoning, it is plain that something at least of M. Brunetière's teaching may be taken to heart by us all. The duty of fitting ourselves not merely to enjoy the great poetry of the world, but to prefer it to all other forms of æsthetic enjoyment, may be insisted upon with advantage. All men will not attain to such enjoyment or such preference; but this is no reason why all men should not be admonished to make the effort to attain. No man follows perfectly the law of Christ; yet no preacher ceases to uphold that law as an ideal pattern of conduct. It is clear, then, that no man or child should be allowed to say complacently, as one so often hears it said, " I don't care for poetry." Perhaps they cannot be made to care for it; but their complacency may at least be shaken.

Again, it is just as certain that there are higher and lower genres of poetry as that poetry is superior, on the whole, to prose. Hence it is our duty to fit ourselves to prefer the higher genres to the lower. This, again, we shall not all attain to. Some people are so constituted that elegiac musings and speculations, such as those that make up the In Memoriam, will always attract them more than the stately march of the Paradise Lost, or the subtle beauty and keen interest of the Divine Comedy. On the other hand, one can find persons who do not care at all for such admirable elegiac verse as Lamartine's Le Lac. In either case, we may be unable to correct the bias; but we need not fail to point out that it is an unfortunate one, if any reliance may and should be placed upon the collective wisdom of the past and the trained judgment of the present.

But our teaching need not stop here. There will always be persons who will care more for the subject-matter of a book than for the style in which it is written; yet we should none the less insist that it is the duty of every man to fit himself to tell a good style from a bad, to enjoy an excellent style, and to eschew, whenever it is possible, the books that are clumsily written. An insistence upon this matter of taste in style has, after many generations, placed French literature in its present position of supremacy: a failure to insist upon it has left German literature where it is to-day. If we Americans and Englishmen will only cultivate our taste for style, and will remember, too, that principle upon which Matthew Arnold was forever harping, that great literature needs a sound subject-matter, we shall all be saved from many bizarre judgments and opinions. We shall not then be able to rank Whitman, true and great poet though he often was, among the *dii majores* of song, nor to imagine that Tennyson or Wordsworth or Shelley can rightly be mentioned in the same breath with Milton.

Yet, although we shall do well to respect the academic critic when he bids us distrust our own judgments and consult the authoritative opinions of the best critics past and present, it does not follow that we must all endeavor to inform ourselves about the evolution of genres, the details of literary history, or any of the numerous matters that assume great importance in the eyes of the professional critic. Few of us have the time for such minute study: fewer still have any inclination for it. One can love and get pleasure from flowers without knowing much about botany; similarly, one can love and get pleasure from literature without being a trained critic. The botanist and the critic, to be sure, ought, unless they become dry-as-dusts, to have decided advantages over the mere lovers of flowers and of books; but the latter are in no bad way if their minds and souls have been enlightened in a broad and general manner. This broad and general enlightenment will begin to dawn upon us the moment we are brought in contact with great literature and art; provided always that our tendency to excessive individualism is checked by proper training. Such being the case, we are in duty bound to range ourselves by the side of those academic critics who offer to furnish this training which, as we have just seen, is by no means technical in character.

V

GRANTING, however, that criticism has a certain authority over us with regard to the submission of our individual judgments relative to such matters as the supremacy of poetry to prose, of one genre to another, of form to formlessness, it would seem to be true also that, as we are constituted with varying tastes and aptitudes, and brought up in varying environments, we are more or less forced to form subjective opinions and thus to become impressionist critics, at least for the time being.   If all criticism is, in its essence, subjective, and attains objectivity only through its subsequent acceptance by minds other than the critic's own, which in turn is a subjective procedure, it is certain that our own judgment or opinion with regard to any object of art will be of more vital importance to us than any conventional judgment or opinion can possibly be.   In other words, the impressionist critic would seem to have a *rôle* as important and a province as extended as the academic critic has.

There can scarcely be two opinions with regard to this matter.   The fact that there are impressionist critics who are widely read and enjoyed seems of itself to prove their usefulness. It is not possible to deny that, by concentrating themselves upon some favorite author, artist, book, or painting, impressionist critics have added to the world's knowledge, and, what is more, to its enjoyment; that they have actually forged weapons for their foes, the academic critics, to use against them. Who, for example, has done more to make contemporary France return to a proper admiration of Lamartine than that prince of impressionists, M. Lemaître? Certainly not M. Brunetière. But impressionists are justified in existing not only by the good they do, but also by the fact that there is an abundant range of work for them to accomplish. There are regions in the domain of literature and art over which the academic critic has little or no control. No one should affirm, for example, that it is the duty of the academic critic to set us rules for the enjoyment or even full comprehension of that department of poetry known as " society verse." He can tell us, indeed, that it should not be ranked high in the scale of the genres; but, if he be wise, he will scarcely undertake to tell us how much we ought to care for it, or when it will most appeal to us.

The reason for this proper reticence on his part is very simple. Society verse does not necessarily appeal to the natural man ; and the academic critic, in most of his reasoning, finds it necessary to give his principles of criticism the broadest basis possible. He tells us that it is human to admire the sublime and to weep at the pathetic; but he cannot tell us with any truth that it is human to smile at the cleverness of a smart social set. The academic critic feels at home, therefore, in praising the Paradise Lost and the Antigone: he will do well to leave to the impressionist — to the man to the manner born, like the late Mr. Locker-Lampson (who indeed could theorize also on the subject in an admirable way) — the task of initiating us into the charming mysteries of society verse. The moment, however, that the impressionist goes too far in his advocacy of his favorite poet or kind of poetry, the academic critic, with his broader knowledge and wider range of thought, is ready to check him. Pope, for instance, is, in many respects, a poet of society whom it would be easy for a certain kind of impressionist to overrate, and for another kind, preferring, let us say, the poetry of nature, to underrate, even to the point of proclaiming that the brilliant satirist was no poet at all. Both these extremes of judgment would surely be corrected by a competent academic critic.

But not only can the impressionist critic serve us as the best possible guide in certain well-defined regions of literature and art; he is also the person to help us in the exploration of new regions. There are genres like the novel, the possibilities of which we are probably far from knowing thoroughly. With respect to present work in these genres, it may be questioned whether the training and methods of the academic critic fit him for doing effective service: he is at his best in dealing with genres of which the capabilities have been long tested. The impressionist, on the other hand, unfettered by rules and traditions, is likely to be sympathetic with the fresh tentatives which creative genius is continually making in what we may call the " unclosed genres." He is the best critic for the new writers and, hence, for the majority of contemporary readers, who naturally form the clientage of the men who are making current literature. Then, again, it is the impressionist critic who is best qualified to apply to the literature of the past those fresh and novel points of view which each advancing generation supplies, — a most important work when it is not undertaken in a captious and self-seeking spirit.

Now surely, if all that has been said be true, the *rôle* of the impressionist is by no means a contemptible one. Not only has he certain departments of art and literature practically under his control, but he can do his share in criticising the men and works of the past, and he has the lion's share of the critical labors of the present. He has no reason to call the academic critic by harsh names; yet he frequently does — seemingly because, being bound by few rules, he forgets that he is bound by any, even by those of courtesy. He generally takes up a favorite and becomes a partisan, after which he fancies that, in order to elevate his hero, he must labor not merely to subordinate, but to cast down other great men. He will praise Tintoretto while belittling Titian; he will laud Shelley while decrying Byron; and he pities the benighted soul that in the bonds and fetters of custom still grovels before the " crumbling idol." This is but to say that, although the *rôle* of the impressionist is a great one, he is often false to it. Narrow and bigoted critics of an academic kind there have been in abundance; and they have done much harm, but scarcely enough to equal that done by the wild impressionists who are forever running amuck through the storied realms of art and literature.

VI

WE are not so much concerned, however, with the failings of our two varieties of critics as we are with the very practical question, how we may get safely steered through the wide sea of literature when so many helmsmen are offering their services; and this question we may perhaps answer in part by summing up the points we have been making.

We have seen already that, in certain matters, we shall do well to rely on the academic critics. We have seen that there are some universal principles of criticism that we should all learn to apply so far as we are able, such as the superiority of poetry to prose, of one genre to another, of form to formlessness. A moment's consideration will show us, furthermore, that corollaries from these principles are easily to be drawn and equally to be observed. Thus, for example, every schoolboy, not merely Macaulay's, should know that Virgil, Dante, and Milton, as great epic poets, are superior respectively to Horace, Petrarch,

and Shelley, as great lyric poets, and should
be ranked accordingly, and that if he does
not like the greater poet so much as he
does the inferior, it is either his own fault
or his own misfortune, which, unless special
reasons to the contrary exist, he should seek
to remedy as best he may.

Within the same category of poetry, however, no such definite assignment of rank is,
as a rule, possible, save when, as in the cases
of Homer and Shakspere, a universal con-
sensus of opinion obtains the force of law.
It is idle, for instance, to assert dogmatically
that Dante is a greater poet than Milton, or
vice versa. Yet nowhere in criticism is there
more tendency to dogmatic utterance than
in this very delicate matter of balancing the
respective claims of two poets of the same
type, whose rank is nearly even; and we
cannot too often remind ourselves that
dogma, although necessary perhaps at times,
is never attractive or satisfactory to the inquiring and aspiring mind. It is open to
us to urge everything we can in support of
our favorite's claims, — the wider acceptance
of Dante and his greater hold upon human
sympathies, or Milton's treatment of the
sublime, and his marvellous metrical mastery, — but, when all is said, when we have

ranged the critics and summed up the arguments *pro* and *con.*, we must frankly admit that there is still room for differences of opinion in this case and in all similar cases.

On the other hand, we cannot too firmly crush out such foolish recalcitrancy against established opinion as was once exhibited by a college student who, when asked whether he thought Bacon could have written Shakspere's plays, replied indignantly, being more in love with philosophy than with poetry: — " Not much ! He would n't have wasted his time on such wretched stuff ! " That young man was not joking, on the principle that a foolish question required a foolish answer: he was merely furnishing an unconscious example of the folly of untrained impressionist criticism.

Other principles of universal, national, and class or individual application might be named that are equally binding upon us and that measure the extent of our reliance upon the academic critic. On the other hand, we have already seen that we should rely on the impressionist for criticism relative to " unclosed genres " like the novel and " non-universal genres " like society verse, to contemporary writers and artists, and to the work of the past in all the genres when it is necessary to reëxamine it from fresh and legitimate points of view. If we will only bear these principles in mind, we shall scarcely go greatly astray in choosing our critics, or in determining how far to follow them.

But if the critics, on their part, continue to assert, as so many of them do, that the average reader has no rights and that art and literature can be truly appreciated only by the elect, the *mandarins*, the public will most assuredly continue to commit its own peculiar absurdities, to consider Tom Jones an immoral book and Ben Hur a great one; to read a thousand copies of Trilby to ten of the Peau de Chagrin; and to rejoice in the flat namby-pambyism of a " native author named Blank " or of a foreign author named Double Blank. And who shall blame them for their eccentricities, when the authority of criticism is so slightly esteemed by nine-tenths of the writers who call themselves critics?

APROPOS OF SHELLEY

II

APROPOS OF SHELLEY

I. INTRODUCTION

IT hardly seems extravagant to say that there is not, in the whole range of English literature, a more entrancing, a more perplexing, a more irritating subject for study and reflection than the life, character, and works of Percy Bysshe Shelley. If any one doubt the truth of this statement, let him spend a few weeks among Shelley's biographers and critics. If he do not read some of the most cobwebby special pleading ever spun, if he do not encounter some of the strangest canons of criticism ever promulgated this side of the " visiting moon "; if he do not find himself now hot with indignation, now cold with shame, now ready to burst with laughter, now ready to weep with sympathy, at one moment in a heavenly glow for the true, the beautiful, and the good, at another longing to assist in sending to the stake every idealist that ever hinted the essential commonplaceness of our everyday life;

if he do not, in short, end by debating with himself whether he is a confirmed dyspeptic or an adjudged lunatic, then he is a most cool-headed and thoroughly enviable person.

But as no one who credits the above truthful record of my own experiences will be likely to enter the enchanted forest of Shelleyan criticism, and as many who have already ventured within its depths may be inclined to tell a different tale, I feel called upon to preface this paper with a few confirmatory excerpts culled from my own reading of the critics, or, to continue the metaphor, I will exhibit a few of the thorns of that enchanted forest that were found clinging to my garments when I succeeded in effecting my escape.

Mr. Carlyle, who would certainly not have owned up to lunacy, although he might have confessed with some propriety to being a dyspeptic, brought away from what was probably a cursory reading of Shelley and his critics, the characteristically formed opinion that the poet was a " windy phenomenon." Mr. Browning, after a profound study of Shelley, wrote of him as follows in Pauline:

" And my choice fell
Not so much on a system as a man —
On one, whom praise of mine would not offend,

Who was as calm as beauty, being such
Unto mankind as thou to me, Pauline—
Believing in them and devoting all
His soul's strength to their winning back to peace;
Who sent forth hopes and longings for their sake
Clothed in all passion's melodies, which first
Caught me and set me, as to a sweet task,
To gather every breathing of his songs :
And woven with them there were words which seemed
A key to a new world, the muttering
Of angels of something unguessed by man."

Years later, in a more mature and nobler poem, perhaps the profoundest poem of the century, Sordello, he wrote these glowing lines:

  " Stay — thou, spirit, come not near
Now — not this time desert thy cloudy place
To scare me, thus employed, with that pure face !
I need not fear this audience, I make free
With them, but then this is no place for thee !
The thunder-phrase of the Athenian, grown
Up out of memories of Marathon,
Would echo like his own sword's griding screech
Braying a Persian shield, — the silver speech
Of Sidney's self, the starry paladin,
Turn intense as a trumpet sounding in
The knights to tilt, wert thou to hear ! "

Certainly there is a difference as wide as the poles between the judgments of the great lay-preacher and of the great poet. Which is right, or are they both expressing half-truths only?

Carlyle and Browning are not, however, professional critics, and it is with the latter that we are especially concerned. Mr. W. M. Rossetti who was asked to write the sketch of Shelley which appeared in the last edition of the *Encyclopædia Britannica* may fairly be called one, and I subjoin a sentence from his very able article:

"In his own day an alien in the world of mind and invention, and in our day scarcely yet a denizen of it, he [Shelley] appears destined to become, in the long vista of years, an informing presence in the innermost shrine of human thought."

Not long after Mr. Rossetti wrote the above delightfully poised sentence Mr. Matthew Arnold concluded what was destined to be with one exception his last critical utterance with the following words:

"But let no one suppose that a want of humor and a self delusion such as Shelley's have no effect upon a man's poetry. The man Shelley, in very truth, is not entirely sane, and Shelley's poetry is not entirely sane either. The Shelley of actual life is a vision of beauty and radiance, indeed, but availing nothing, effecting nothing. And in poetry, no less than in life, he is 'a beautiful *and ineffectual* angel, beating in the void his luminous wings in vain.'"

Here is a sentence for us as neatly turned as Mr. Rossetti's, as positive in its expression of individual opinion, and proceeding from a far greater hand. But we must contrast this again with Mr. Swinburne's vehement dictum that Shelley is "the master singer of our modern poets," and must then remember that neither Wordsworth nor Keats, both of whom had great tact and discernment in all matters relating to their art, could appreciate Shelley's poetry.

Nor is the case different with regard to Shelley's life, or with regard to his character and acquirements. As good and clear-headed a man as Charles Kingsley thought him a far less lovable character than Byron, while Byron, cynic as he was, declared that Shelley was the most gentle, the most amiable, and least worldly-minded person he ever met. As it was in his life-time, so it is now and probably ever will be — a most difficult matter to determine from the verdicts of his critics alone whether he was a spawn of Satan or a seraph of light. I have the impression that I have somewhere seen him styled an archangel, and I am certain that

not many years ago a distinguished Southern divine consigned him, in the course of a
sermon, to the horrors of everlasting flames,
in company with another picturesque subject
for damnation, Edgar Allan Poe.

In view of all these diverging opinions we
are hardly surprised to discover that critics
are not quite agreed as to the position to be
accorded Shelley as a philosopher. We find
one of his biographers describing him as " one
who lived in rarest ether on the topmost
heights of human thought "; but Mr. Leslie
Stephen, who is an authority in such matters,
would hardly seem to recommend the rarity
of this ether when he writes: " In truth,
Shelley's creed means only a vague longing,
and must be passed through some more philosophical brain before it can become a fit
topic for discussion." A vague longing, one
opines, can be had by a dweller in the hum-
blest valleys of thought.

But the biographers who track Shelley to
these heights of rarefied atmosphere seem
to succumb to the attenuating influences of
their environment and to take very rarefied
views of actions which in our grosser atmosphere we are wont to call by very gross
names. Here are some samples.

It seems to be pretty well agreed, even by

Shelley's warmest admirers, that the poet's utterances about himself and his surroundings cannot always be accepted with implicit faith — in short that Shelley not infrequently, whether consciously or unconsciously, did not tell the truth.   But mark how Professor Dowden, with the approbation of another biographer, Mr. Sharp, deals with this little failing. Says the Dublin professor: He "was one of those men for whom the hard outline of facts in their own individual history has little fixity; whose footsteps are forever followed and overflowed by the wave of oblivion, who remember with extraordinary tenacity the sentiment of times and of places, but lose the framework of circumstance in which the sentiment was set; and who, in reconstructing an image of the past, often unconsciously supply links and lines upon the suggestion of that sentiment of emotion which is for them the essential reality."

Now, although I believe that in Shelley's case Professor Dowden has not strayed far enough to lose all sight of the truth, I submit that the above sentence rarefies facts in a way that should commend itself to the heart of every lawyer with a guilty client to defend. Such a lawyer should also take to heart the judgment of Mr. Sharp with regard to his hero's conduct to the unfortunate Harriet, "that Shelley, intoxicated with vision of the ideal life, behaved unwisely, and even wrongfully, in his conduct of certain realities."

Is it any wonder, I may be permitted to ask, that an ordinary mortal like myself should be glad to escape from the jungle of Shelleyan criticism, or that I should feel impelled to stop every one I meet, like an Ancient Mariner but with a less potent eye, to point my moral and adorn my tale? In pursuance of this task, whether it be imposed upon me by vanity or fate, it will be necessary for me to pass in review biographical facts that have been discussed thousands of times, and poems that every one knows by heart or by critical report. Yet this is the lot of all who venture to write about famous authors, and I should not regret it were it not for the fact that I labor under the unpleasant consciousness of knowing that sooner or later, I must bring up in a camp defended by only one stout soldier, that I must fight on under an unpopular flag, that I must cut myself off from leaders to whom I have always looked up with reverence and admiration.[1] Nevertheless I " cannot choose " but speak even though I may not

[1] Especially from my friend Dr. Richard Garnett, whose devotion to Shelley is so well known.

be able to compel a single wedding-guest to hear me out while I say my say about Shelley, the man and the poet.

II. LIFE AND CHARACTER.

As the experiences of life must furnish the materials upon which both the imagination and the fancy work, it is always interesting and important to know at least the main facts of a poet's life. This is especially true in the case of Shelley, whose life and whose poetry are, to use a word of which he was inordinately fond, inextricably " interpenetrated." The main facts of this life are fortunately beyond dispute, but the judgments to be passed upon these facts are unfortunately very far from settled. I say the main facts, for it is surely of little importance for us to know whether Shelley was really attacked and fired upon by a burglar at Tannyrallt, or whether he was simply suffering from a fit of hallucination consequent upon a too copious draught from his laudanum bottle, the facts of his susceptibility to hallucinations and of his use of laudanum being sufficiently attested in numerous other instances. We have an abundance of consentaneous testimony as to the poet's personal idiosyncrasies, and about such facts as his desertion of his first wife there is unfortunately no doubt whatsoever. But as these facts are familiar to most persons who are at all interested in literature, it will be sufficient here to indicate briefly what seem to me to be the chief conclusions one ought to draw concerning Shelley's life and character.

The first point that strikes one is, I think, the utter absence of all that is spiritual and elevating and refined from Shelley's early environment. Upon this point, Mr. Arnold lays great stress in the essay that has already been quoted from, and it is a most important point. There probably never was a child who would have responded so readily as Shelley to ennobling and purifying influences, there never was a child who so entirely missed them. There is hardly a trace of any maternal influence; and his sisters were too young and too much accustomed to worship their eccentric but most kind and lovable brother, to make any serious or sobering impression upon him. His father was a typical English squire of the period, who has been rather harshly treated by his son's biographers. If he was dull, conservative and somewhat servile to the powers that be, he was only what his environment made him, and was no better or worse than thousands of his contemporaries were then, or than some English squires doubtless are to-day. Nor are such characters at all confined to England, for one may meet many a Mr. Timothy Shelley in this progressive and enlightened country of ours. But it was a deplorable fact for Shelley that he had such a father, and certainly Mr. Timothy Shelley thought that it was a deplorable fact for him that he had such a son.

Now a sensitive, high-strung boy, who could not find good influences at home, was hardly likely to find them at Eton or at Oxford during the early part of this century. Public schools and universities exercise an admirable influence upon normal or only slightly abnormal youths, but they never did and never will suit natures such as Shelley's was; and sensible parents should have recognized the fact. Shelley picked up much curious information, of course, during his school life, which served him in after years, but he did not learn what is the best thing that schools and colleges teach, to use his common sense. It is a very great mistake to think, as so many do, that our school days are set apart to enable us to use what may be called our uncommon sense; the main duty that lies before every child in his school days is to learn to use his common reason on common things, and it is the main duty of his teacher to see that he does it. But none of Shelley's teachers seems to have seen or done his duty in this regard toward him, and they have in consequence suffered at the hands of his biographers. Only one has practically escaped censure, the venerable and kindly Dr. Lind whom Shelley idolized and whom he has immortalized as Zonanas in Prince Athanase, and the hermit in Laon and Cythna. Now, while not meaning to disparage Dr. Lind's kindness, I must record my conviction that he is one of the most unwholesome influences connected with Shelley's early life. I long believed that I was the only person in the world that held this opinion, until I found that Mr. John Cordy Jeaffreson maintains it with great vigor in his able but unfair biography of the poet, the question-begging title of which (The Real Shelley) ought to warn off the uninitiated. My charge against Dr. Lind is simply this, — that, having gained a strong influence over his impressionable pupil, he failed, so far as the records show, to use that influence to any good purpose. We know, indeed, that he encouraged Shelley in that fondness for thin and cloudy metaphysical discussion which was afterwards to lead to his expulsion from Oxford, to his sins as a mystifying rhetorician when he should have been writing divine poetry, and finally to his being labelled by practical, or rather would-be practical men like Carlyle, " a windy phenomenon." We know also, that he encouraged Shelley to dabble in science, which was about as bad as encouraging him to dabble in metaphysics. If he had taught Shelley to love science with the wholesome thoroughness of a sound mind impressed with her wonders, he would have conferred an inestimable boon upon him. As it was, he gave him a fatal bias toward dabbling that affected his whole after career, and furnished Matthew Arnold an excuse for labelling him with that terrible adjective *ineffectual*. Dr. Lind seems to me to have been the only man who had a chance to set Shelley's feet upon the paths of common-sense, and I believe that had he tried he could have become a saving and corrective influence to one of the noblest but most erratic spirits that ever " lighted upon this orb which " he " hardly seemed to touch." How much English poetry, and so the whole world, would have profited by this influence, cannot be estimated. But Dr. Lind's talent has long since been removed from its covering napkin, and it is by no means certain that I have not done him grave injustice by coupling his name with the undesirable notoriety that attaches to the slothful servant of the parable.

I must pass over Shelley's Oxford career in spite of the fascination which Hogg's description thereof must always lend to it. As at Eton, he found no one to guide him, no one to sympathize with him save Hogg, who, though commonsense and practical enough in some respects, and though devoted to Shelley, was hardly the proper person to correct his extravagances. Certainly the dons who drew up their sentence of expulsion before they had given the youthful atheist a chance to exculpate himself, simply fitted in with the rest of his soul-cramping environment. They were doubtless honest enough, however, in their belief that Shelley was fast speeding to the devil and endeavoring to drag his sleepy University with him, and the young visionary was probably more contumacious than his friend Hogg has seen fit to record.

One could wish one might pass over with equal rapidity the few years that connected Shelley with the unfortunate Harriet Westbrook, but it cannot be done. In those years was to be gathered the first bitter fruit of his reckless and ill-trained youth; and in those years the Muse of English Poetry had to bewail the marring and almost total undoing of what promised to be the purest, the most beautiful spirit that had ever been born to do her service. But if one cannot pass over these years, one may at least presuppose that every one is familiar with the harrowing facts on which one has to base one's judgments and one can give those judgments briefly.

Shelley, as we all know, had by this time broken completely with the past. He had dabbled in science natural and occult, had carried his metaphysical speculations to the verge of absurdity, and had announced that he loathed history. He had overleaped all prejudices of caste and become a radical in political and social matters. Being the most sincere and courageous of mortals, having in him the stuff of which the martyr and the hero are made, loving his fellow-man with all the intensity of his nature, ever aspiring toward what he believed to be the true, the beautiful and the good, he was not likely to share the fate of most young enthusiasts of twenty, to sow his wild oats and settle down into a well-to-do, conservative man of family, a smug and contented *laudator temporis acti*. What Shelley believed, that he would do, and hence the pitiable necessity under which his friends and relatives labored of teaching him what to believe. But what had Mr. Timothy Shelley, what had the Oxford dons, what had Mr. Thomas Jefferson Hogg, finally what had dabbling Dr. Lind to teach this genius of a youth who could pierce their commonplace theories of religion and politics and social life as easily as an eagle can pierce the web of gossamer which an adventurous spider has woven over its nest? And what had the times to teach him? for when a youth cannot be taught by his intimates, he sometimes finds in the writings of great contemporaries or in the march of the world's progress lessons of the highest import to his inquiring soul.

The times taught him precisely what his own spirit felt naturally toward its environment — revolt, self-sufficiency in its best sense, aspiration. The forces of the French Revolution had by no means spent their strength. In spite of Napoleon, men were everywhere dreaming of liberty and of the glories that awaited the enfranchised spirit of man. The world was severed from its hateful past and history was now of less value than the visionary dreams of any self-appointed prophet. Kings were ˎbut creatures set by Providence upon thrones for the sons of liberty to take a savage pleasure in overthrowing them. The giant custom was to be slain by a pebble from the sling of some philosophic David; religion, law, morality were to be annihilated or metamorphosed, and a new heaven was to look down upon a new earth. Such was the Zeitgeist whose wings fanned the forehead of Shelley and it was against the breathings of this spirit that the wingless words of Mr. Timothy Shelley and his like had to contend.

But if sober wisdom was not to flow in upon Shelley from his contemplation of the world's mad vortex, he was in still less likelihood of obtaining it from the lips or from the pens of his contemporaries. Although he was not unfamiliar with the great writers of the past these could not have influenced him very profoundly, simply because they belonged to that past which the present seemed determined to break with. We of this generation can see that if he could have been brought under the spell of Burke, there might have been some salvation for him; but Burke was at a discount among fiery enthusiasts in 1812. Instead of Burke Mr.

Timothy Shelley recommended Paley, at the mention of whom our young poet fairly foamed at the mouth when he ought merely to have smiled. Paley *versus* Shelley savors somewhat of the ridiculous, as Mr. Arnold intimates.

But to whom else could he apply? Wordsworth, it is true, had written most of his best poetry and Shelley had read it, but was not Wordsworth, too, bitten by the revolutionary frenzy, and did not Shelley address him a very mournful sonnet when the elder poet began to show signs of increasing conservatism? Southey too he had read and liked — but could Southey help him, especially after they became personally acquainted? Could Coleridge have helped him as he afterwards claimed that he could? Were Walter Scott's delightful poems likely to contain the antidote to revolutionary views, or the youthful poems of Byron? No — there was not one living author in England who could have done him good, but there was one who did him infinite harm.

It would not profit us to consider here how the thin speculations of William Godwin attained their astonishing vogue, or to analyze those speculations, interesting as the task would prove. Godwin was a man of undoubted talents, as any one that has read Caleb Williams or St. Leon will admit, and the impossible anarchistic and free love theories of his " Political Justice " were certainly presented with no little power. They were just such theories as suited the visionary, sympathetic, and revolutionary youth who had outraged his father and his teachers; and when Shelley took up a theory he acted on it except when he could see plainly that it hurt another. Nor could Shelley take up a theory without endeavoring to make proselytes to it, and so we see his star surely and by inevitable necessity drawing into its orbit that milder star that was soon to be lost to the sky — the star of the unfortunate woman whose name is forever linked with his.

But why pursue the harrowing story? Could the ill-sorted union of a revolutionary young aristocrat destitute of common sense and a half atheistical, half evangelical young female of low extraction and romantic aspirations have any other ending than that cold grave in the Serpentine? Blame Shelley as much as we will — and he deserves blame — we shall still find back of the whole sad story just what we shall find back of the expulsion from Oxford, back of his sickening love affairs, back of every foolish and uncanny action of his life, that terrible lack of common wisdom which results always, or nearly always, from an unpropitious environment.

But when Shelley separated himself from Harriet, did he find the environment he needed? How could he with Godwin for a father-in-law — Godwin ever whining and begging, a most grasping philosopher in spite of his doctrines of equality — with poor Fanny Imlay (Mary Shelley's half sister) committing suicide for love, it is said, of her poet brother-in-law — with Jane Claremont and her unhappy intrigue with Lord Byron — with Byron himself plunged in dissipation and sick of life? Some of these were, we may suspect, worse for him than Harriet's sister, that Eliza with the pock-marked face and the shock of hair, who kept all the money of the establishment in her own pocket, whom Shelley first loved and finally execrated in the following language: "I sometimes feel faint with the fatigue of checking the overflowings of my unbounded abhorrence for this miserable wretch."

This is a little strong even when it is written about a sister-in-law. Poor Shelley — he was always, to use a homely metaphor, jumping from the frying-pan into the fire with regard to the " company he kept," especially the women. At first sight his new acquaintances are divine, in six months they are made of the commonest clay. Who will ever forget that Miss Hitchener with whom he began a platonic correspondence, whom he persuaded to break up her school and take up her residence with him and Harriet, whose praises he sounded under the poetic name of Portia, though she was really Eliza the Second, whom finally he wound up by calling the " Brown Demon " and by bribing her to leave his house. Was such a man sane?

But Shelley did make one great, one inestimable gain by his connection with Godwin. He gained a noble and sympathetic woman for his wife — a woman who was to share his trials, soothe his wounded and weary spirit, and finally after his death to plead successfully with a cold world for his memory. This was much more than he had a right to ask, and so his last years were far happier than he had any right to expect. Indeed after the soul-harrowing struggle which he made to retain his children by his first wife, throughout the whole period of his second visit to Italy, Shelley's environment was in most respects all that his better nature could have desired. Byron grew to love him and so avoided shocking him or exerting much, if any, deleterious influence upon him; the Williamses, the Gisbornes, Medwin, Trelawny, Peacock, Leigh Hunt were pleasant companions, and Mary Shelley was the noblest of wives. But for the silly episode of Emilia Viviani, these Italian days of Shelley were as sunshiny and pure as Italian days should ever be. He was maturing in his powers, had refined the crudity of many of his earlier theories, and with renewed health might have looked forward to accomplishing work that would have thrown in the shade his previous labors in song, when by an unhappy accident, or perhaps a despicable crime, he was sent to meet his death in the bosom of that element he had loved so well.

But we have assuredly dwelt long enough on Shelley's unfavorable environment, and we are, some of us, doubtless prepared to admit with Mr. Arnold that Shelley was not entirely sane. We shall hardly look upon him as a spawn of Satan, but we shall wish that he could have been blessed with more common sense. There is, however, another side of Shelley's life and character which we have as yet only glanced at and which we must now consider at more length, although we can by no means give it the attention it deserves.   Unless we bring this side into view, we shall fail to comprehend at all how Shelley has come by his many admirers, perhaps I should say, his many worshippers.

As I have already stated, Shelley was one of the most fascinating and lovable of men. Even his bizarre and uncanny peculiarities strengthened the charm that he exerted on cynics like Byron, cool commonsense persons like Hogg, dilettante natures like Hunt, and pure, sweet enthusiasts like Mary Godwin. But Shelley's charm did not proceed from his eccentricities, or from the magic of his conversation, or from the glow reflected upon him from the enchanted atmosphere of fanciful thought and feeling in which he moved habitually. Shelley's charm came from the essential simplicity of his character, a statement which will appear paradoxical to those who have been chiefly struck by the complexity of the problems connected with the poet's life. They will recognize at once that it is a paradox, for nothing can be more clearly established than the fact that Shelley's was an essentially simple nature. And by simple I mean, of course, *sine plica*, without a fold, a straightforward nature aiming to put itself in harmony with the universe, not a doubling, dissimulating nature, in spite of

Mr. Jeaffreson's charges and of Shelley's own inconsistencies of statement, never in perfect harmony even with itself. Shelley's nature can be summed up in one word — love. He loved man in the most thoroughgoing sense of that great and often misused word "philanthropy" — he loved beauty whether in woman, or flower, or wave, or sky, or in the creations of art, or in the abstractions of the human mind. But a simple, perfect love does not dominate the world of thought alone, it dominates the world of action also. Hence Shelley's whole life was given up to deeds of love, to obeying the promptings of the spirit that swayed him. But mark how the very nobility and simplicity of his nature betrayed him when he sought to put it into action, how it led his sun-fed and light-sustained body through the thorns and briers of life. Every action implies a subject and an object, and for an action to be good it must be in harmony with the essential nature of both subject and object. Yet how is the subject to know that an action which is in entire harmony with it will be in entire harmony with the object toward which it is directed? There is no possible way of arriving at this knowledge except the rough way which we call gaining wisdom or common sense. Some natures seem, indeed, to have an intuition of the rightfulness or the wrongfulness of actions, and to them Wordsworth refers in his noble Ode to Duty as

" Glad hearts without reproach or blot
Who do thy work and know it not."

But this intuition will not answer long in our jarring world, and Wordsworth recognizes the fact when he prays : —

" Long may the kindly impulse last;
But thou, if they should totter, teach them to
stand fast."

The duty, however, which Wordsworth prays to cannot well be separated from what we also know as wisdom and, under humbler circumstances, as common sense. Shelley, therefore, if he was to obey the promptings of the spirit that swayed him — that exquisite spirit of love with which he was more completely " interpenetrated " than any other child of man has been in these latter days—needed of all men to have wisdom to guide him in his actions; because being so conscious of the purity of his own motives, he was the less likely to pause and consider whether his actions would redound to the good of his fellow men and women. Here, alas! was the rock on which Shelley split — he had no common sense, he had little practical wisdom, certainly in his earlier years, and he had an uncontrollable longing to follow the impulses of his nature. What wonder that he wrecked his life in whirlpools, what wonder that in his own beautiful, self-depicting words —

> " He fled astray
> With feeble steps o'er the world's wilderness,
> And his own thoughts, along that rugged way,
> Pursued, like raging hounds, their father and their
> prey."

It is this inability of Shelley's to regulate his actions that Mr. Arnold refers to when he speaks of Shelley's lack of humor and his self-delusion. Shelley was always pursuing the true, the beautiful, and the good, and since he had not wisdom to guide him, he was continually thinking that he had found those desirable qualities embodied in some one person who sooner or later turned out to be an idol of clay. Having imagined that Emilia Viviani embodied them, he must forsooth become her slave and write that wonderful Epipsychidion in which he declared that she was the sun of his life, while his faithful and noble wife, Mary, was the moon. He did not stop for a moment to think that what he had written affected two women injuriously — making one silly woman sillier, and rendering a true and deserving woman temporarily unhappy. So it was with the unfortunate Harriet. Shelley could not see that the theories which were for the time true for him, were very bad theories with which to inoculate a by no means strong-minded girl of sixteen. Nevertheless, he proceeds to inoculate her, marries her without loving her, deserts her because he has found the true, the beautiful, and the good embodied in Mary Godwin, and then invites her to come and live with Mary and himself because he has no idea that he has done anything wrong. He has simply followed the promptings of the spirit he served, but he has followed them without exercising his common sense. In other words he has shown a lack of humor, a self-delusion that are astounding.

But there are often times when a lack of humor and a self-delusion that are astounding do not prevent a man like Shelley from moving like an angel among his fellow men. Think of him visiting the huts of the poor at Marlow, tending the sick, distributing money and food to them, actually walking a hospital that he may learn for their benefit something of practical medicine. Think of the ophthalmia caught in his constant ministrations to the sick, think of his subscriptions to public charities, think of his sweet treatment of the importunate Godwin, think of his sympathy for every living thing, man or beast, and then say if your heart does not glow toward this man. Even his rash pilgrimages for the emancipation of Ireland cease to be ridiculous when we remember the noble love of liberty that prompted them, when we remember that many of the reforms he proposed have been since carried out by the peaceful means he advised. We have, of course, to set against this ideal, angelic Shelley, the silly, almost demoniac Shelley raging at kings and statesmen and priests with a wearisome iteration. But this uncontrolled hatred of customs and institutions that most men cherish was but another manifestation of Shelley's spirit of love uncontrolled by wisdom. Love for mankind was for him inextricably bound up with love for liberty, and love for liberty with intense natures means hate for tyranny; but Shelley had not the wisdom to see that too often what he called liberty was simply license. Hence his ravings and hence our paradox that his hatred of kings was only a manifes-

tation of his spirit of unbounded love.
But a spirit of unbounded love will have
worshippers to the end of time.

This subject has fascination enough, however, to keep us pursuing it indefinitely, and
we may as well pass on. It is impossible
to compass even the salient points of
Shelley's life and character in an essay: but
it is to be hoped that we have done enough
to enable us to approach his poetry in a
sufficiently critical but at the same time
friendly mood.

III. THE POEMS.

In discussing Shelley's work as a writer it
will be well for us to confine ourselves to
his original poetry. If this were a treatise
instead of an essay it would not be difficult
to devote more than one chapter to setting
forth his merits as a translator of poetry and
as a writer of distinguished and charming
prose. We need not yield even to Mr.
Arnold himself in our admiration for Shelley
in these two capacities, although we may
not share the great critic's opinion that it
is as a translator and a prose writer that
posterity will chiefly appreciate one who is

very frequently styled at present "the poets' poet."

I know of nothing in the realm of poetical translation that approaches the delightful and inimitable Hymn to Mercury or the equally inimitable, though to me less charming, scenes from the masterpieces of Calderon and Goethe. Nor do I suppose that in its way Shelley's nervous prose with its individual rhythm and its almost invariably sound and sane content can easily find an equal. When he abandons himself to the looser measures of rhythmic prose, when his inspiration ceases to master him and he masters his own genius, he displays a tact, a sureness of touch that almost make us forget the lack of wisdom and of grasp upon reality that are so painfully apparent in his life and, I may add, although this is somewhat forestalling matters, in his original poetry. But no translator, no prose writer, however distinguished, can claim the place in literature that is always ungrudgingly assigned to the eminently original poet, and Shelley's worshippers have never been willing to forgo pressing his claims for the higher place. Here is the true crux of Shelleyan criticism, and it is to the question of Shelley's position as an original poet that for the present at least the energies of his critics must be directed.

To a superficial observer the question would seem, at first sight, if not to have solved itself with time, to be at any rate in a fair way of doing so. Shelley's star has been steadily rising ever since his death. In his life he found few admirers, and Byron, Moore, and even many whose names are now almost forgotten, eclipsed him in critical as well as in popular favor. Soon, however, his admirers became more numerous and bolder. The uncanny events of his life were viewed in a soberer and fairer light, and his work received more impartial criticism. The sun of Byron began to pale before the rising sun of Tennyson as after a period of revolution and stormy passions the world began to sigh for the peace of conservatism and the luxury of allowing play to calm emotions and delicate sensibilities. This desire for calm and the liberty and equality which had been made an influential aspiration, if not an achieved possession, of the human spirit, produced a type of civilization characterized by many distinctively feminine traits. Gentleness, receptivity to sentiments and ideas, a recognition of the virtue and power that lie in patient forbearance and pathetic weakness, these and many other distinctively feminine traits began to dominate the world and have continued to dominate it. Naturally the effects of this change of the world's spirit were seen in literature, and Tennyson's Princess may be taken as its first fairly adequate expression. But obviously this change was in favor of Shelley and to the detriment of Byron. The poet of stormy passions, of intense, over-weening masculinity, was out of touch with this new world; the poet who preached love to man and beast and flower, who spun rainbow-hued visions of the speedy advent of a golden age of harmony and peace, whose character even, when closely examined, was found to be in many respects that of a feminine angel — if angels may be said to distribute themselves between the sexes — became more and more a subject for veneration and love to the advanced and enlightened spirits of the new régime. The populace took to Tennyson and Longfellow, but the critics and the ultras of all shades took to Shelley, with here and there an æsthete who preferred Keats, or some more ambitious prober of mysteries who gave his allegiance to Browning. Then came the Pre-Raphaelite movement in painting and poetry which naturally worked in favor of a hazy poet and under the influences of which the best of our younger critics have been reared.

So the fact appears to be that time is settling the value of Shelley's poetry for us, since if the critics cleave to him long enough, they will eventually bring the people to him. It is seldom that an author remains indefinitely balanced between critical appreciation and popular indifference. Landor seems to hang thus suspended, but as a rule either the people will bring the critics to their view of the matter, as in the case of Bunyan, or the critics will educate the people to a more or less willing acceptance of the views of the enlightened, as seems now to be the case with Browning. If the critics as a class continue to stand by Shelley, his cause may fairly be considered as won. But although such a stout phalanx as Swinburne, Dowden, Sharp, the Rossettis, Saintsbury, Symonds, Woodberry, Garnett, Myers, Forman, Stopford Brooke, Theodore Watts-Dunton, Andrew Lang, Thomas S. Baynes, and a host of others, to say nothing of the Shelley Society, has stood by and is still standing by Shelley, there is one voice of dissent that makes itself heard, a voice potent enough to arrest our attention and to awaken our interest. It is the voice of the greatest English critic of this century, with the possible exception of Coleridge, Mr. Matthew Arnold.

But what is one man against so many, one will ask? Not much, I answer, for the present, but a great deal for the future if he happens to have truth on his side, and if he has recorded himself with sufficient fulness; for the value of the rest of his critical work is bound to lend some authority to his most extreme utterance even when this seems to be opposed to the judgment of the wisest of his contemporaries. It is the voice which is at first drowned in the discord of dissent or censure that in the majority of cases is heard full and clear by the generations that follow. Can we be sure that this will not be the case with Arnold's utterances as to Shelley? For my part, even if I had committed myself as a pronounced Shelleyan, even if I had written a commentary in the most approved modern style on a single passage in the works of my favorite, I should still deep down in my heart feel a dread of the future when I listened to the clear yet calm voice of such a dissenting critic as Matthew Arnold. And his uniqueness, the fact of his standing alone, of his unflinching boldness of utterance would increase the dread, for it is just such unique and bold utterances that in nine cases out of ten win the suffrages of posterity. At any rate, being no pronounced Shelleyan I propose to give Mr. Arnold a more respectful hearing in the following pages than he has usually had at the hands of modern critics.

Before proceeding, however, to examine Arnold's views it may be well for us to remember that he was not handicapped in his criticism of Shelley, as Kingsley was, by his own more or less intimate dependence upon the established order of things. Arnold was, if not as blatantly, nevertheless as completely at discord with orthodox Christianity as Shelley was. It is open to grave doubt whether he believed in the immortality of the soul, which Shelley certainly did. Arnold was also a republican at heart and a believer in equality, even if he did not rave against kings and statesmen with conservative leanings. He was furthermore a product with Shelley, though a more ripened product, of the liberal, the European movement in literature which received its initial impulse from Goethe. He was therefore not unqualified either by nature or by training to sit in judgment upon Shelley.

APROPOS OF SHELLEY

It would not be possible nor would it be desirable to cite here all Arnold's *obiter dicta* respecting Shelley's poetry — he did not live to write his promised essay about it — hence I shall content myself with quoting three passages from his writings that set forth his views with sufficient fulness, reserving my own discussion of Shelley's poems until we have felt the full force of the most weighty indictment that has been brought against them.

A lucid statement of one of Arnold's chief charges against Shelley as a poet occurs in the essay on Maurice de Guérin:

" I have said that poetry interprets in two ways; it interprets by expressing with magical felicity the physiognomy and movement of the outward world, and it interprets by expressing with inspired conviction the ideas and laws of the inward world of man's moral and spiritual nature. In other words, poetry is interpretative both by having *natural magic* in it, and by having *moral profundity*. In both ways it illuminates man; it gives him a satisfying sense of reality; it reconciles him with himself and the universe. . . . Shakspere interprets both when he says,

" 'Full many a glorious morning have I seen
Flatter the mountain-tops with sovran eye;'

and when he says,

> " 'There 's a divinity that shapes our ends,
> Rough-hew them how we will.'

. . . Great poets unite in themselves the faculty of both kinds of interpretation, the naturalistic and the moral. But it is observable that in the poets who unite both kinds, the latter (the moral) usually ends by making itself the master. In Shakspere the two kinds seem wonderfully to balance one another; but even in him the balance leans; his expression tends to become too little sensuous and simple, too much intellectualized. The same thing may be yet more strongly affirmed of Lucretius and Wordsworth. In Shelley there is not a balance of the two gifts, nor even a coexistence of them both, but there is a passionate straining after them both, and this is what makes Shelley, as a man, so interesting: I will not inquire how much Shelley achieves as a poet, but whatever he achieves, he in general fails to achieve natural magic in his expression; in Mr. Palgrave's charming *Treasury* may be seen a whole gallery of his failures."

To this passage Mr. Arnold added a foot-note contrasting Shelley's Lines Written in the Euganean Hills with Keats's Ode to

Autumn as follows: " The latter piece *renders* Nature, the former *tries to render* her. I will not deny, however, that Shelley has natural magic in his rhythm; what I deny is, that he has it in his language. It always seems to me that the right sphere for Shelley's genius was the sphere of music, not of poetry; the medium of sounds he can master, but to master the more difficult medium of words, he has neither intellectual force enough, nor sanity enough."

Passing over other interesting but not especially important references to Shelley, we come to the concluding paragraphs of the noble essay on The Study of Poetry which was prefixed to Ward's " Selections." Arnold has been speaking of the wholesomeness of much of Burns's poetry and suddenly he exclaims with a warning voice: " For the votary misled by a personal estimate of Shelley, as so many of us have been, are, and will be — of that beautiful spirit building his many-colored haze of words and images

'Pinnacled dim in the intense inane'

no contact can be wholesomer than the contact with Burns at his archest and soundest." And he proceeds to point his warning by contrasting four lines from the " Prometheus Unbound with four lines from Tam Glen.

Finally from the Essay on Byron we may take our last quotation: " I cannot think that Shelley's poetry except by snatches and fragments, has the value of the good work of Wordsworth and Byron. . . . Shelley knew quite well the difference between the achievement of such a poet as Byron and his own. He praises Byron too unreservedly, but he felt, and he was right in feeling, that Byron was a greater poetical power than himself. As a man, Shelley is at a number of points immeasurably Byron's superior; he is a beautiful and enchanting spirit, whose vision, when we call it up, has far more loveliness, more charm for our soul, than the vision of Byron. But all the personal charm of Shelley cannot hinder us from at last discovering in his poetry the incurable want, in general, of a sound subject matter, and the incurable fault, in consequence, of unsubstantiality. Those who extol him as the poet of clouds, the poet of sunsets, are only saying that he did not, in fact, lay hold upon the poet's right subject-matter; and in honest truth, with all his charm of soul and spirit, and with all his gift of musical diction and movement, he never, or hardly ever, did . . ." The rest of this passage containing Mr. Arnold's praise of the translations and prose works need not be cited, but it may be remarked that it is at the close of this essay on Byron that the famous phrase which has been already quoted first occurs: " Shelley, beautiful and ineffectual angel, beating in the void his luminous wings in vain." When some years after he had occasion to repeat this phrase Arnold underscored the word *ineffectual*.

And now I think we can form a pretty plain idea of the nature of the charges that his greatest critic has made against Shelley's poetry. If they are not ruthless, they may certainly be termed vital. If Arnold is right, Shelley cannot be a great poet of the highest rank. We see also that Arnold's charges may be summed up very briefly. Shelley's poetry does not show moral profundity though it shows a straining after it; it does not show natural magic in its language although it does show it in its musical rhythm; it lacks a sound subject-matter and hence is characterized by the incurable fault of unsubstantiality. This is the sum and substance of Arnold's criticism, and the important question for us now is — can this criticism be deemed just? There is only one way to test it and that is to read Shelley's chief poems in the light or the darkness of Arnold's *dicta*, and then sum up our fresh impressions and form our judgments accordingly. It would be better still if my reader were able to do as I did — viz., re-read all Shelley's poems several years after reading Arnold's strictures and then re-read the strictures in the light of the poetry. Few probably who have done this will find themselves so nearly in accord with the critic as I did, and fewer still will in reading The Revolt of Islam rediscover Shelley's lack of natural magic in his language without sufficient recollection of Arnold's essay to enable them to give their rediscovery a proper name. But now let us turn to the poems themselves, omitting the juvenile works and beginning with Alastor.

Many critics go into ecstasies over this semi-autobiographic effusion and some of us when sound delighted more than sense, probably went wild over it ourselves. Now unfortunately the opening lines are too plainly suggestive of Wordsworth; the famous passage beginning:

> " His wandering step
> Obedient to high thoughts has visited
> The awful ruins of the days of old :
> Athens, and Tyre, and Balbec, and the waste
> Where stood Jerusalem "

is grand, but with the grandeur of Milton not of Shelley; the straining after an impossible ideal is pathetic but not stimulating, and the whole atmosphere of the poem is unreal, as unreal as the poet's geography. Alastor is chiefly interesting for two reasons — it is autobiographic and Shelley is an interesting character and it has a fine, I may say, at times a superb and original rhythmical flow. But a poem autobiographical of Shelley could not well be sane — could not have a sound subject-matter, could only embody a straining after moral profundity, which is but to confirm Arnold's sure judgment. It is its rhythm only that lifts it out of the mass of immature poetry in which our literature is rich, and Arnold is not backward in his praise of Shelley's rhythm. Alastor may be dismissed so far as specific criticism is concerned, with the remark that the charge so often made against Byron that he only paints himself, can be made fully as justly against Shelley, and that Byron at least describes a strong personality, Shelley a weak although a pathetic one.

This judgment, which I confess sounds harsh and irreverent, but is made in all soberness, may be illustrated by a recurrence to the famous if somewhat twisted dictum of

Milton that poetry should be simple, sensuous, impassioned. Alastor, and indeed all Shelley's other elaborate poems, fail of simplicity because simplicity implies a sound subject-matter treated by a sound mind and inevitably appealing to all other sound minds. Our analysis of Shelley's character, however, forbade us to hope for any such simplicity in his poetry, for we saw that his environment had failed to give him that wisdom which would have directed his essentially simple nature whether in its actions or in its poetical self-delineations.

Alastor and Shelley's other poems are sensuous in one respect — their rhythm, which can be proved by any one with an ear for poetic rhythm and which justifies Mr. Swinburne in saying that Shelley is "the master *singer* of our modern poets" and Mr. Arnold in speaking of Shelley's genius as being peculiarly suited to the sphere of music. But little of Shelley's poetry is sensuous in its language — that is Shelley as a rule does not by a single felicitous epithet, phrase, or verse set a concrete object or an abstract quality vividly before the mind's eye. Shelley needs a mass of words to produce his effects — hence the haziness of his descriptions, which nevertheless have at times just the beauty that haziness in the natural world generally gives.   Hence it comes that Shelley loves to give us clouds and sunsets and impossible landscapes, hence it is that few great painters have ever, to my knowledge, been inspired by him, and hence it is, that comparatively few quotations from his poems are familiar to ordinary readers.   Even a eulogist like Mr. John Addington Symonds has to admit this, although he does not give the reason for it, when he quotes Shelley's famous lines from Julian and Maddalo,

> " Most wretched men
> Are cradled into poetry by wrong,
> They learn in suffering what they teach in song."

Even here, it is interesting to note, Shelley is nothing if not autobiographic.

But finally, to return to Milton's dictum, Alastor and the rest of Shelley's poems are impassioned, yet only in the lowest sense of the word.   Shelley's was the passion of weakness but not the passion of strength.   Here is the true cause of his essential inferiority to Byron; here is the reason, as Mr. Richard Holt Hutton well showed, why Shelley's poetry is not sublime.   There is no sublimity without power and Shelley's power was only the pseudo-power which morbid and introspective people can discover in weakness. We do speak, it is true, of sublime patience and the like, but the collocation of terms is an unfortunate one except in those cases when there is involved with the patience the power of acting effectually if the sufferer choose. In other words, it is difficult not to agree with Mr. Hutton that there can be no sublimity without power, and it is clear that the power that accompanies patience is rarely the positive power of action but only the negative power of restraint. But all Shelley's ideals were passive — he even preached passive revolutions — hence his poetry is not truly impassioned, it does not flow from a powerful nature or affect other natures powerfully — that is, it tends to excite sentiment rather than to incite to action.

The above criticism of Alastor applies as well to the beautiful poem known both as Laon and Cythna and as The Revolt of Islam. Most people tire of this poem, because of its impossible, misty and rather wearisome plot. Even professed Shelleyans share this feeling, and while pointing out the beauty of a few detached passages frankly admit that Shelley had no qualifications for the rôle of a narrative poet. We need qualify this judgment only by saying that in all likelihood Laon and Cythna is the most continuous stream of exquisite and delicate melody ever poured upon the ears of the world since Spenser left the Faërie Queene unfinished. Of its kind I know nothing like it in any language — but its kind I must confess is musical, not poetical. As poetry it is as full of flaws as any poem of a real genius ever was, as music, as a song without concrete meaning, it is simply wonderful. It may be remarked that in the 34th stanza of the 11th canto of this poem we find one of the few examples of a truly felicitous, a naturally magical epithet used by Shelley. Such an epithet is so rare that it must be quoted, with the caution, however, that it perhaps contains a reminiscence of Dr. Donne.

> " Thus Cythna taught
> Even in the visions of her *eloquent* sleep."

No other adjective could well equal the one which Shelley has here used; in other words it is inevitable, *i. e.*, truly poetic. But, if it is seldom that one can quote such a perfect epithet from Shelley, it is not difficult to quote many a stanza to prove his perfect melodiousness. Here is one.

> " She moved upon this earth a shape of brightness,
> A power, that from its objects scarcely drew

APROPOS OF SHELLEY

One impulse of her being — in her lightness
Most like some radiant cloud of morning dew,
Which wanders thro' the waste air's pathless blue,
To nourish some far desert: she did seem
Like the bright shade of some immortal dream
Which walks, when tempest sleeps, the wave of life's
    dark stream."

As poetry this is feeble because there is scarcely a word that clinches the object it is intended to represent or describe, but as music it is little less than divine.

Passing over Rosalind and Helen with the remark that it is feeble as a whole, and less good in its parts than Shelley's poems are wont to be, we reach the celebrated Lines Written among the Euganean Hills. These I like better than Mr. Arnold did, although I recognize that they are far less artistic than Keats would have made them. I recognize also Shelley's indebtedness to Milton and perhaps to Dyer. But I must plead that the apostrophe to Venice has a combination of epic and lyric grandeur that is rarely surpassed and that deserves a grateful remembrance. One may note, however, that both in this poem and in the famous Hymn to Intellectual Beauty which follows it, there is that note of despairing weakness which is so characteristic of Shelley.

Going for a moment past The Cenci, we come to what is considered by many of his critics to be Shelley's most important work — Prometheus Unbound. The language that has been applied to this lyrical drama would certainly not be too weak in connection with The Tempest of Shakspere or the Comus of Milton. Mr. Sharp speaks of "The wonderful melodies, the splendid harmonies, all the music and magnificence of Shelley's greatest production." Mr. Rossetti is still more enthusiastic when he grows eloquent over "The immense scale and boundless scope of the conception; the marble majesty and extra-mundane passions of the personages; the sublimity of ethical aspiration, the radiance of ideal and poetic beauty which saturates every phase of the subject, and almost (as it were) wraps it from sight at times, and transforms it out of sense into spirit; the rolling river of great sound and lyrical rapture" — and so forth. Mr. J. A. Symonds went so far as to declare that "a genuine liking for 'Prometheus Unbound' may be reckoned the touchstone of a man's capacity for understanding lyric poetry." On the other hand it is to be observed that the only passage of Shelley, so far as I remember, that Matthew Arnold undertook to condemn specifically came from the Prometheus Unbound and that it would be rash to maintain that a poet who had written such lyrics as Arnold was not capable of understanding lyric poetry.

The truth seems to me to lie very far this side of the unbounded praise that has just been recorded. Not that there is not some foundation for this praise, but that it is plainly extravagant. It strikes what Arnold calls somewhere the note of provinciality, the note of shrill assertion that that which we like is perfect and that whoever does not like it is a fool. I shall not at all quarrel with Mr. Sharp's " wonderful melodies " and " splendid harmonies," for they surely exist in the poem; but I should like to point out that not only does the poet's love for singing songs without sense often mar his work, but that his facility of utterance often tempts him to strike what is clearly a false note, as for example the lines quoted by Arnold beginning:

"On the brink of the night and the morning."
or what to my mind is an even worse instance of a thin false note, the chorus of spirits in the fourth act, beginning: —

> We come from the mind
> Of human kind

> Which was late so dusk, and obscene, and blind ;
> Now 't is an ocean
> Of clear emotion,
> A heaven of serene and mighty motion.

This is not only rendered feeble as poetry from its straining at concrete expression, but it is also rendered thin and of false quality as music because the rhythm does not harmonize with its content. It hardly seems extravagant to say that there are more false notes struck in the Prometheus than in the rest of Shelley's poems taken together.

With regard to what may be called the intellectual claims put forth for this poem which has been edited for schools and been made the subject of essays by the dozen, I can say only that, however true they may be when applied to special passages, they are by no means true when applied to the drama as a whole. The fourth act, which is a favorite with the Shelleyans, seems to have been an afterthought, and is a most lame and impotent conclusion. The characters are, except for short intervals, vague, misty and devoid of personality. The solution proposed for the problem of human destiny, for the freeing of the Promethean spirit of man is as impossible and ineffectual as if it had been generated in the heated brain of a maniac. This great poem is really little more than a series of wonderful phantasmagoria flashed forth upon the curtain of the reader's mind by a very unsteady hand. When the reader voluntarily shuts off the light, *i. e.*, ceases to think or judge, the effect is dazzling; when he allows the light of reason to play upon his mind, the effect is just the reverse. I admire the Prometheus Unbound as the daring and in parts splendid achievement of a brilliant, unbalanced, but nobly poetic nature; but I cannot admit that it is worthy of language which would be hyperbolical in the case of any other poet than Shakspere or Milton.

But to hasten on. With Prometheus there were published in 1820 at least four poems that have assuredly won immortality — the Ode to the West Wind, The Cloud, The Sensitive Plant and To a Skylark. Some would add to these the Ode to Liberty, but I cannot, if for no other reason, on account of the metrical insufficiency of its stanzaic form. It is needless for me to attempt to characterize poems which have seized the world's heart; but I must point out that to my mind Shelley is in one of these and in many of his other lyrics more a poet of the fancy than of the imagination — of most subtle and beautiful fancy, I admit, but still fancy. The Cloud, it seems to me, will prove the truth of this remark. Arethusa may also be cited in support of it. It is trite to say, however, that the odes To the Skylark and The West Wind display in parts superb imaginative power. The closing lines of the latter:

> "O, Wind,
> If Winter comes, can Spring be far behind?"

are richly imaginative; the stanza of the former that runs:

> " What thou art we know not;
> What is most like thee?
> From rainbow clouds there flow not
> Drops so bright to see
> As from thy presence showers a rain of melody,"

is richly fanciful. It is to be noted that in nearly all these poems, there is an undertone of weakness, of despair.

Passing over Swellfoot the Tyrant with the remark that it is easy to agree with Mr. Symonds in disparaging the mass of Shelley's political, satirical, and avowedly humorous poetry, including The Masque of Anarchy, and that uncalled for metrical fungus Peter Bell, the Third, we come to the famous Epipsychidion, which may be likened to the sacred dimly-lighted shrine, in which the ritualistic votary of the high-Shelley-church party worships with the greatest unction, leaving the profane and uninitiated herd of Shelleyans to carry on their devotions in the more spacious and lofty cathedral of the Prometheus Unbound. I have already referred to this poem as occasioned by Shelley's sudden and soon abandoned passion for Emilia Viviani, and I have pointed out the painful deficiencies of the production from the point of view of morals. I fully agree with those critics, however, who see in it a wonderful intensity, a white heat of passion. But I have seen intense heat in a burning pile of decayed leaves, and I am not certain that the heat of this poem does not remind me more of burning leaves than of an ever burning sun. Shakspere's sonnets show passion at its intensity, but their heat is like the heat of a burning sun. Yet the description of the isle to which the poet urges his new found love to fly with him is, if unearthly, nevertheless the most wonderful thing of its kind that one need ever expect to read — exquisite fancy and a perfect sense for melody were never so thoroughly fused and ignited by emotion as in this passage.

As for Adonais, who would touch that

most melodious of elegies with a rough hand? Certainly its subject matter is sound even if unsubstantiality be a characteristic of its author's treatment. Certainly it has the natural magic of sound to perfection, if not that of language. Certainly it will live to couple together forever the names of two noble poets. But just as certainly it has not the sure, the inevitable touch of the master hand upon it, the touch that Milton's hand gave to Lycidas. Hellas, too, who would wish to be ruthless with, even if many professed Shelleyans do speak of it with little rapture? The fragments of its prologue are wonderful and far sounder, far saner, far more powerful, and therefore nearer to the sublime, than anything in Prometheus Unbound. Of course, we all know that Shelley's energy gave out and that Hellas remained a fragment — a noble fragment, however, containing the most satisfying of all the poet's numerous choruses: the chorus that contains such a stanza as this: —

> " Another Hellas rears its mountains
> From waves serener far;
> A new Peneus rolls his fountains
> Against the morning star.
> Where fairer Tempes bloom, there sleep
> Young Cyclads on a sunnier deep."

How much truer, how much more satisfying is this than the love-making of the earth and the moon in the vaunted fourth act of Prometheus?

Putting aside Julian and Maddalo, a poem of the Rosalind and Helen, order, only more successful, the fragmentary Prince Athanase, the impossible but superb metrical freak of The Witch of Atlas, and the charming Letter to Maria Gisborne, which shows what Shelley with his delicate fancy could have done in the delightful realm of society verse, we come full upon the mass of fragments and short lyrics which in my judgment represent Shelley's chief contribution to literature. But before discussing these, I must say a few words about that remarkable drama The Cenci.

I call it remarkable because it is perhaps, the most completely objective piece of work ever done by a subjective poet. Shelley saw plainly that he must efface himself, if he would succeed as a dramatist, and he did it most effectually. But something more than the effacement of one's subjectivity in the construction of a drama is necessary to its success. Shelley did not efface himself in his choice of theme, possibly no dramatist can —and not being a sound, wholesome character, he failed to choose a sound, wholesome theme. But Ford and Webster and Massinger chose unwholesome themes and succeeded. This was because they were greater dramatists than Shelley, because they had their genius more under control, because they knew human nature better. Not a single character in Shelley's play is a real human being, except Beatrice, and she lacks the charm which a greater artist would have given her, in order to counteract the horror with which her environment and her actions invest her. Beatrice is strong and noble, but she is hardly flesh and blood, and I am not sure that Shelley does not cause her to fall in our esteem, when he allows her to use her power to make her unfortunate accomplice eat his words in order that she may preserve the honor of her family. Remembering the poet's description or representation of that family, one is forced to ask how any honor could be left to preserve. I cannot pursue the subject, save to add that in only one or two passages, especially in the closing lines, do we strike a note of true poetry, or even of true music. But a tragedy without here and there a deep poetical note is like a desert without an oasis. Imagine the Duchess of Malfi stripped of its poetry! This fact alone makes the opinion of those critics idle who claim that The Cenci is the greatest tragedy since Shakspere. I suppose they mean the age of Elizabeth, for I can hardly imagine a discreet person's putting Shelley's work beside that of Webster or Ford. But even if they mean this, they overshoot the mark, for Otway with his Venice Preserved, and his Orphan has to be reckoned with, to say nothing of Dryden and Byron.

But now let us conclude this long, this much too long paper with a few words about Shelley's fragments and lyrics. What can English poetry show to equal them of their kind? and what is their kind? I answer simply — the lyric of weakness, of longing, of despair. We are all weak at times, we all have longings, we all despair, and so it is that Shelley's " lyrical cries " take hold upon us, and fascinate us, and never leave us. Let us think them over and see if we have not analyzed truly the secret of their fascination — the Invocation to Misery, the Woodman and the Nightingale, The Indian Serenade, Love's Philosophy, I fear thy kisses, gentle maiden, To the Moon, Time Long Past, the Dirge for the Year, To-night, Time, Music, when soft voices die, Rarely, rarely comest thou, Mutability, A Lament, Re-

membrance, One word is too often pro-
faned, Ginevra (though this is not a lyric),
The Recollection, with its

> " Less oft is peace in Shelley's mind
> Than calm in waters seen,"

the dirge beginning " Rough wind that moan-
est loud " — why, the very titles almost give
one the " blues," so sad they are. Yes, here I
think we have the secret of Shelley's power
over us all; but, as I remarked before, it is
a misnomer to speak of power in this passive
sense. Shelley is like an Æolian harp — the
winds of his sad fate play upon him and immortal, weird, sad, and haunting melodies
float away to us and enter our souls and
abide there. And we love the harp — and
some unthinkingly worship it, and who shall
blame them?

It is true that among these fragments and
poems many pieces can be found that show
real power — many that have not a trace of
weakness or sadness; and it is instructive to
note that these pieces were mainly composed
during the happy years in Italy when Shelley's
powers were rapidly maturing. Had he been
spared, there is no telling what he might
not have done. I have already referred to
the power displayed in the Prologue to Hellas, and although I cannot praise the Tri-

umph of Life, as Shelleyans are wont to do, I am by no means blind to the power of that. The Ode to Naples is to my mind a much more magnificent poem. One can hardly praise it too highly. And where is the beauty of joy more fully set forth than in the famous bridal song beginning—

"The golden gates of sleep unbar."

But words are weak and ineffectual when we deal with such fragile and delicate things; all one can do is to quote them, yet I have no space for that and they are too well-known. I will merely quote two stanzas of a not very familiar poem, as worth in my opinion, on account of their true ring, all the hazy paintings of sunsets and clouds that Shelley ever gave us. They occur in the poem addressed to Mary Wollstonecraft Godwin:

> "Upon my heart thy accents sweet
> Of peace and pity fell like dew
> On flowers half dead; thy lips did meet
> Mine tremblingly; thy dark eyes threw
> Their soft persuasion on my brain,
> Charming away its dream of pain.

> "We are not happy, sweet! our state
> Is strange and full of doubt and fear;
> More need of words that ills abate —

APROPOS OF SHELLEY

> Reserve or censure come not near
> Our sacred friendship, lest there be
> No solace left for thee or me."

Here, I venture to think, there is a wholesome subject-matter, and a natural magic both of sound and of language. For Matthew Arnold, though right in the main in the criticisms he passed upon Shelley, might, one would think, have somewhat modified his famous formula. Shelley is by no means "ineffectual," although his elaborate work probably is in part. He is not a poet of sovereign and sustained endeavor like Milton and Spenser, he has not the moral profundity of Wordsworth, he has not the sure touch, the exquisite art of Keats, or the passion and the mastery of Byron, but he is the most musical, the most sympathetic, the most aspiring spirit that ever succeeded in saving itself by means of its sylph-like wings from the ever greedy and onward rolling waves of the oblivious ocean.

III

LITERATURE AND MORALS

III

LITERATURE AND MORALS

I

So much use has been made in recent years of the formula "Art for art's sake" that it seems almost an impertinence to drag it forward again for purposes of discussion. Yet the relations of literature to morals form a theme of such perennial and transcendent interest that nearly any critic is warranted in making them a basis for his lucubrations, and whenever these relations are in question, the convenient but often misapplied formula simply has to be reckoned with, since all literature that is worth considering is plainly the product of a specific art.

In its most commonplace application the formula means merely that art does not exist primarily for purposes of preaching or teaching—which is a contention that will displease no one who has the slightest idea of what art is or rather what it does. The primary object of every art is to appeal pleasurably to the emotions which we denominate æsthetic, that is those that affect chiefly the eye and the ear

— and as neither preaching nor teaching has such an appeal in view, except indirectly as a means to an end, it follows that art cannot be true to itself if it preaches or teaches of set purpose. Pure art, in other words, exists only for purposes of æsthetic gratification, and whenever any artistic product gives us gratification of another sort, it is either because the emotions of the artist were not purely æsthetic or because we find it impossible to put ourselves in a condition of receptivity in which our æsthetic sensibilities are alone brought into play.

It is hardly necessary to remark that there never has been in all probability a perfectly pure artistic product or a man or woman capable of receiving perfectly pure æsthetic pleasure. Our emotions, whether we act as creators or recipients of such pleasure, are too mixed for such a consummation. It is necessary to remark, however, that it by no means holds that pure art is *per se* nobler and of greater value to the race than mixed art, that is, art that appeals to mixed emotions. There are other emotions besides the strictly æsthetic, to wit the intellectual and moral, and the latter, which we may for convenience assume to include the spiritual, have long seemed to most men to be the noblest emotions humanity is capable of feeling. A work of art, while appealing primarily to the æsthetic emotions and taking its artistic as differentiated from its other characteristics from the fact that it makes this appeal, may, in its inevitable appeal to other emotions, so pleasurably affect our highest spiritual nature as to gain immensely in nobility through the very fact that it is not a pure artistic product but a mixed one. Examples are not wanting to illustrate the truth of this contention. The Mona Lisa undoubtedly gives its beholder supreme æsthetic pleasure, but it would not be so great a picture as it is if it did not give him also the spiritual pleasure of seeking to establish relations of sympathy and amity between his own soul and that which lurks inscrutable in the depths of those disillusioned but divinely benignant eyes. In literature Poe's Ulalume gives us, perhaps, an example of the *ne plus ultra* of purely æsthetic appeal to ear and eye through its wonderful rhythm and its supernatural shadowing, but what sane critic would contend that Poe's weird poem is nobler than the less purely æsthetic Elegy Written in a Country Churchyard in which Gray succeeded in stirring the moral emotions of humanity to a degree rarely surpassed?

It is just here that we can put our finger on the most dangerous use that has yet been made of the formula " Art for art's sake." Critics and artists by the score have assumed that pure art is necessarily more to be desiderated than mixed art, and have of late tended steadily not merely to stress technique in the interests of what we may call art-isolation, but to be suspicious of the criticism which concerns itself at all with the moral and intellectual aspects of art, and even to eschew subjects that might strongly suggest such criticism. Some of them go farther yet and maintain that as art exists primarily for the purpose of giving æsthetic pleasure, the artist should not be hampered in his choice of subject by any other than æsthetic considerations. As we have just seen, it is, to begin with, an absurd hypothesis to suppose that any subject can be chosen that will make a purely æsthetic appeal; and even if this were the case, it would not follow that an artist would be justified in throwing to the winds the advantages gained by choice of a subject furnishing high moral and æsthetic pleasure at one and the same time. We may readily grant that in choosing his subject the artist usually and rightly bases his choice upon æsthetic considerations and that in a majority of cases his selection is spontaneous rather than determined upon principle, but it rarely happens that after he has begun his work he remains totally unconscious of the moral bearings of his subject, and there are surely some subjects that involve important moral considerations the moment they suggest themselves to the mind. The painter who chooses to paint a repulsive woman in a repulsive attitude cannot claim the right to retort "honi soit qui mal y pense" to his censorious critics. We should make all due allowance for the unconscious element in art, but if we once admit that it is our duty — as it surely is — to order all our actions upon the highest plane possible to us, it follows that the artist who aims for purely æsthetic effects is, if conscious, guilty of a moral lapse, and, if unconscious, guilty of a grave error, whenever it can be shown that his work would possess higher value for the race were its subjects so chosen as to appeal also to our moral and intellectual emotions. We cannot therefore accept that extension of the famous formula which leads people to hold that the moralist and the thinker are guilty of impertinence when they ask to be represented on every jury of artistic awards. To pursue an art primarily for the purpose of preaching

through the medium of communication it
offers between soul and soul, is to degrade
two noble functions of human genius; but to
pursue an art in total oblivion of its relations
with thought and morals is always to hamper
and often to degrade art alone, since thought
and morals will under all circumstances retain
their dignity. Positing then as the basis of
our reasoning the contention that the formula
" Art for art's sake." does not, when properly
interpreted, make for art-isolation, and con-
fining ourselves hereafter in the main to a
consideration of literary art proper, let us see
what light can be thrown upon the relations
borne by literature to morals by treating the
subject from the threefold point of view of the
relations to morals sustained by the writer,
the reader, and the written work.

II

THE primary object of the literary artist is
to give expression to his æsthetic emotions in
such a way as to communicate them to others,
but if, as we have just seen, the literary product is sure to cause other emotions as well,
and if most people read more or less pas-
sively, we must conclude that, in the majority

of cases at least, these other emotions were consciously or unconsciously imparted to the literary product by the artist.[1]   In some cases, however, it is obvious that the intellectual and moral emotions caused in us by the perusal of a piece of literature are mainly due to the fact that there are secret connections between the centres of such emotional forces and the æsthetic emotions created by the literary product.   Over these secret connections the writer has plainly no control, for he cannot gauge the emotional capacity of each several reader; he is therefore responsible only for such intellectual and moral stimulation as he experiences himself when engaged in creating his literary product, and this responsibility can be measured only on the assumption that there is an emotional standard fitting the normal man.   It is a commonplace of criticism that the richer a writer's emotional nature is the more emotively effective his work will be, hence it follows that if it be our duty to make the most of our talents, it is incumbent upon every literary man to develop his moral and intellectual nature to the utmost in order to make himself an ideal artist and thus a supreme power for good, provided always that he pre-

[1] See *post*, Essay II., p. 156, note.

serves his artistic poise. From this point of view at least the relations of the writer, as of every other creative artist, to morals, are as clear as they are difficult to sustain in a proper manner, but they are also, as we easily perceive, the same that every conscientious man sustains, merely as man.

It would seem that we have arrived at the conclusion that a great writer must be a very good man, but fortunately or unfortunately — we need not stop to determine which — such a conclusion is not warranted either by our process of reasoning or by a careful study of literary history. Lord Byron, to take only one instance, was not an exemplary man, but even his most aggressive modern detractors are hardly inept enough to deny that he was a great writer, although they come as near as they can to doing it. The cant which seems to be an essential component of the Anglo-Saxon nature, makes many of us anxious to establish the relation of cause and effect between personal goodness and literary greatness, but although noble names like those of Scott and Longfellow help us, such names as those of Swift and Poe prove awkward stumbling-blocks. We have simply omitted to consider the fact that goodness has little meaning when used of a person unless it

refers to conduct, whereas emotions, which
are essential to artistic creation, need not
translate themselves into conduct at all. It
may indeed be held that really noble literary work cannot be done by a man incapable
of noble conduct, but the noble writer need
not be an actually noble man. His emotions
may exhaust themselves in his artistic creations, and his conduct may be ignoble in the
extreme. Then again so great is the force of
artistic sympathy that it might be possible
for a writer of objective literature to simulate
or actually feel for the time being noble emotions he had observed in others but never
felt in his proper person, just as it was possible for Shakspere, reversing the process, to
give us Iago and Richard III.

There is a further fact that we neglect to
consider when we try to establish the contention that the truly great writer must be a
really good man. This is the fact that the
intellectual qualities of literature while not
vastly important in determining its value can
by no means be overlooked. These are the
qualities, rather than moral and æsthetic
ones, that make writers like Swift and Pope
such great literary figures. It is needless,
however, to remark that intellect and good
conduct are not causally related.

But while we are estopped from believing that the literary artist must be a good man in order to win genuine success, it remains perfectly true to maintain that every moral and spiritual advance made by a writer in his conduct ought to increase the richness of his emotional life and thus to make him a nobler literary artist, provided always that his artistic impulse is strong enough to resist the antagonistic desire to give himself up to a life of spiritual contemplation or activity. The poetry of Tennyson and Browning is all the greater for their spiritual experiences; but that of the latter gains over that of the former for the reason that Browning's nature did not become so unbalanced as Tennyson's and never led him to withdraw from society and thus to deprive his poetry of that element of adaptation to the psychical needs of struggling humanity that does not always emerge from the polished verses of his more popular contemporary. It cannot be doubted that Byron's work need not have lost in energy, which is its most vital characteristic, and that it would have been far richer, had his spiritual life been led on a higher plane — on the plane, for example, to which his enthusiasm for the cause of Greek freedom was conducting him when the fatal fever cut short the most fascinatingly brilliant career that any Englishman has had, perhaps, since the days of Drake and Raleigh. On the other hand the Middle Ages furnish us the example of a period when spiritual forces were too strong to allow many men to attain the artistic poise necessary to effective creative work; and the pathetic career of the Irish novelist Gerald Griffin who gave up the chance of becoming an Irish Sir Walter — in order to do the silent work of a pious priest, as Mr. Aubrey de Vere has touchingly reminded us in his late volume of Recollections, serves to indicate that from the point of view of art at least a man's spiritual emotions and aspirations may be too intense.

The artist who is lost to the world because he has devoted himself to the work of priest or philanthropist can cause us only a partial regret which may be richly atoned for; but what are we to say of the artist who instead of rising above the spiritual level consistent with artistic poise falls below that required of all intelligent men? There surely is a spiritual level which the average man of thought and action is expected to keep under penalty of being censured by his fellows if he fall below it; yet we are gravely told that a painter may paint and an author write regardless of the consequences that may flow from his work, provided only that he satisfy the æsthetic demands of himself and a coterie of connoisseurs. A man, so we are told, may write a story that is not merely unspiritual but positively antagonistic to all that is regarded by normal men as spiritual, without rendering himself liable to reproach provided his style be exquisite, his powers of characterization good and his narrative faculty above reproach. All life is his province, and as the lascivious, the base, the brutal are elements of life, he is at liberty to make such use of them in his work as may please his artistic self. Now surely this is a bold demand to make — one that would not be made for any other class of mortals. We even demand of the successful general in time of war that he shall repress brutality among his soldiers; but we encourage some novelists to glorify brutality and vulgarity whenever we hasten to buy their books. We stand aghast at the proposition that all life is the artist's province because we do not see at once where a line can well be drawn, and are yet certain that unless the proposition be qualified, the highest and purest features of our civilization may be endangered by the vagaries of irresponsible men of genius. But if we will only view the matter calmly, we shall perhaps find a way out of our dilemma without being compelled to deny that life is indeed the province of the artist in general and of the writer in particular.

Our loophole of escape is a very simple one, so simple indeed that we continually fail to find it — so simple too that we have a right to blame the artist who does not make it plain to us. All life is the artist's province, but what gives life represented in art its value to the artist and to ourselves is what we may term its emotional content. The artist observes some phase of life emotionally and consciously or unconsciously transmits his emotions to us along with a representation of whatever caused them. If his emotions are pure, we shall be profited, under normal circumstances, by being allowed to share them. We have a right to demand that all emotional appeals made to us shall be pure and pleasurable, and we may make this demand of the writer or plastic artist just as legitimately as we may of our friends and acquaintances who indeed are sometimes obliged on account of the exigencies of life to make demands upon our sympathy that cannot be pleasurable to finite beings. Furthermore it is the duty of every man to obtain as pure, pleasurable, even spiritual emotion as he may from his daily life and experience, and this duty is especially incumbent upon the artist on account of his high endowment. It is his duty to look upon life with pure, spiritual eyes, as it were, and if he does this, his emotions connected with any manifestation of life will be pure and spiritual and will not lose this character when after having been embodied in a specific work of art they are transmitted to us who are brought into subtle relations with the latter. Hence we conclude that the artist may indeed take all life for his province but that he must also see to it that he represents artistically no phase of life that does not give him pure emotions which he may transmit to us. But when we feel repelled by his treatment of a special phase of life, what is it but a proof that, from our point of view at least, his emotions were not pure and high and that he himself was consciously or unconsciously below a proper spiritual level when he was engaged in the inception and completion of his artistic product. And when a sufficient number of cultured men feel thus with regard to the work of any writer, painter, sculptor, or musician, who shall deny that they have as much right to consider such an artist as morally delinquent as they have to judge any individual of their acquaintance whose conduct has shown that he has not maintained himself at the spiritual level properly to be demanded of him? We cannot indeed draw any hard and fast lines in such matters, but society would be in a bad way if no man could be judged save by hard and fast rules, that is by positive law civil or canonical.

We are thus led to conclude that just as the artist as artist must not rise above such a spiritual level as will be consistent with his continuing to make art his life work, so he should not fall below such a spiritual level as will fit him to be a proper companion for true and good men in all lands and in all ages. Perhaps we may express these truths epigrammatically by saying that the modern artist ought never to be an ascetic recluse, and ought always to be a thorough gentleman. We make no greater moral demands upon him than we do upon other men, save in so far as his endowment makes him more responsible to his own conscience and to society; but we certainly shall not, if we are wise, give him more license in matters moral and spiritual than we give other men. It is the constant fault of those who preach art-isolation that they demand license rather than liberty for the artist; but the great public has never really given in to their contentions, and the great public is right.

I am aware that this may sound very philistine; but I am quite ready to take the consequences. I cannot see how the man of genius can claim extraordinary privileges; I see only that he labors under extraordinary responsibilities and that more rather than less in moral and spiritual matters should be demanded of him. This phase of our discussion cannot, however, be regarded as closed until we have considered the moral responsibilities of the reader or recipient of artistic pleasure; for if we may make demands upon the artist, he may surely make reciprocal demands on us. But it is only when we fail in our duties toward the artist that the charge of philistinism properly lies at our doors, hence my nonchalance with regard to the possibility of lodging such a charge successfully against what I have just been saying. It is no failure in duty toward the writer or painter to insist that each shall be a gentleman in his emotions; it would rather be a failure in duty toward each not so to insist.

But while it is easy to scout the imputation of philistinism, it is unsafe to incur the charge of obscurity, and it may therefore be well to illustrate the train of thought we have been pursuing. Two fruitful sources of dissension between the public and the world of artists and critics have been the representation of the nude in plastic art and the treatment of the problem of sex in fiction. There has been a great amount of philistinism displayed on the public side, much of it in America, as the fantastic sallies of Mr. Anthony Comstock and the prudish mincings of certain gentlemen of Boston plainly show; but this we shall discuss later. There has also been much bravado displayed by the authors and critics, and both parties to the controversy have in consequence frequently lost their tempers. But surely the problem is not so difficult as it has generally been considered, if we view it in the light of what may be called the theory of the emotional basis of art. A nude picture which a true artist is impelled to paint because of the pure æsthetic, intellectual and moral emotions that come to him when he contemplates the divine beauty of the human form cannot possibly cause other than pure, wholesome emotions in any normal person. When it does, the spectator who is offended is simply giving play to his idiosyncrasies, and in this connection it may be proper to remark that a whole people may become more or less idiosyncratic when a one-sided movement, intellectual and spiritual, like puritanism, dominates it for a long period of time. The English-speaking peoples are all more or less idiosyncratic with regard to this matter of the nude in art, and whenever any one among us is displeased by all or nearly all representations of the nude, it is a sure sign that such a person is of a nature far too warped for him fairly to claim to be considered as forming part of the public that has the right to judge an artist.

On the other hand it is indisputable that there are many representations of the nude which satisfy critics from the point of view of technique but are felt to be repulsive by persons who have no bias against the nude in art. What does this mean if not that the artist while revelling in true æsthetic emotions during the creation of his work, was also dominated more or less by emotions the reverse of moral or spiritual — emotions which were transferred to canvas or marble and thence to the spectator with the result of disturbing the latter's spiritual balance and causing him disquietude in proportion to his purity of soul? It is no escape from this conclusion to point to the art devotees who profess to enjoy the picture or statue free from disturbing qualms. These people render themselves unfit judges through the very fact that in posing as judges they have tended to stress one set of emotions, the purely æsthetic, as those which alone are to be taken into account by critics of the plastic arts. Having wilfully blinded themselves to the intellectual and moral aspects of art, they quite naturally go into ecstasies over the most ambitious picture in the new portion of the Luxembourg, and fail to understand how a spectator who has stood in adoration before Titian's glorious recumbent Venuses in the Tribune of the Uffizi should feel uncomfortable in the presence of the powerful but coarse canvas of the Frenchman. This phenomenon of criticism is of too frequent occurrence to be dismissed with a trite "honi soit" or a commonplace about the necessity for technical training, or a shrug of the critical shoulders; it does not admit of being explained by the imputation of philistinism or of being passed lightly over with a careless "de gustibus non est disputandum." It is an important phenomenon that challenges attention and that is plainly explicable in the light of the theory of the emotional basis of all art.

The same reasoning holds with regard to

the treatment of the problem of sex.   The novelist has a clear right to use this as an element of his story, provided only that he treat it as a gentleman should.   The idea that the novel must be made suitable to a school-girl is too ludicrous to warrant discussion, but the idea that the novel must answer the requirements of pure-minded men and women is one that should be present to every writer of fiction.   It will not do for one instant to say that a novelist may be so interested in his characters and situations that he may depict them in any way that does not violate the canons of artistic probability.   It is incumbent upon him to view life as a pure-minded, clean-hearted man of genius.   This point of view attained, his emotions will inevitably be fit for translation into an artistic product that will offend no normal reader whose idiosyncrasies are held under control. It goes without saying that in respect of idiosyncrasies we English-speaking peoples are less fortunate than the French.   We could produce a Scott, — but it will be many a long year before we have our Balzac.   On the other hand it cannot be denied that the French have been too lax in the control they have put upon their novelists.

They have not demanded pure emotions

and pure work from their writers of fiction, and thus have rarely obtained the latter except when, as in the case of Balzac, the noble character of the novelist was the safeguard of his literary creations. We may leave this phase of the subject with the remark that Mr. Hardy's Tess of the D'Urbervilles is an excellent novel to be used as a test of the truth of our contentions. This great book was subjected to a hue and cry on the part of squeamish readers both in this country and in England, but it arrested and held the attention of the judicious through the fact that the novelist's emotions were strong and pure whatever one may say of the strictly intellectual appeal of his strenuous story, or of its utilitarian value as a plea.

It now remains to make one important qualification with reference to all that has been said — a qualification that will lead us easily to the next stage of our discussion, the relations to morals sustained by the reader.

The terms " moral " and " spiritual " as we have continually applied them, must be taken in their most general sense if they are to have any meaning or value. To say that a writer must be capable of spiritual emotions is not to say that these emotions can be labelled specifically as Christian, or Mohammedan, or Buddhist. They will be emotions that enter into the warp and woof of every religious life, but they will be emotions that Marcus Aurelius and Epictetus felt just as truly and perhaps as profoundly as St. Augustine and St. Bernard. The reason for this is found in the fact that it is of the essence of art that it should aim at a universal appeal, and it is enabled to make this appeal only through the fact that it interprets universal life in connection with universal emotions — that is, with emotions shared by all normal men. It would be as much a profanation for the artist, who is the apostle of beauty, consciously to limit his appeal, as it would be for the scientist, who is the apostle of truth, or for the priest, who is the apostle of righteousness. It goes without saying that as we have produced, in letters at least, only two universal artists, Homer and Shakspere, artists as a class have not been any more faithful to their ideals than have the various peoples to whom they have appealed, and that it is therefore admissible to speak of pagan and Christian art and to discuss the spiritual qualities of the work of the respective classes of artists in terms of the specific religion that dominated them. It goes without saying too that the more completely the world accepts Christian teachings in one form or another the more completely will the terms "moral" and "spiritual" as they have been used in this discussion be synonymous with the term "christian" when it is applied to the emotions. At present, however, we cannot fault an artist if his morals and his spirituality have reached the stage common to good men in every clime and of every religious faith. We may, however, find it natural to be more closely drawn to those artists whose emotions are "spiritual" in our own more intimate sense of the term. There cannot, however, be the least excuse for a sectarian interpretation of the term "spiritual." Christianity is catholic in its aspirations and hence the phrase "Christian art" is not a misnomer; but a sectarian or even a puritan art would be things to smile at, could they ever exist. John Milton was a great artist, not because he was a puritan, but partly in spite of it. It is well to note, however, that while the artistic spirit is distracted by dissent, it is smothered by intolerance.

III

THE relations sustained to morals by the reader or by the recipient of æsthetic pleasure in general may be considered from the three-fold point of view of his duty to the writer or artist, to himself, and to his fellow men at large.

It may fairly be said that very few readers pay any attention to the first duty. They are forever thinking of what a writer owes them, but seldom of their reciprocal obliga-tions. Yet it is plain that these obligations exist. It is clear that as a writer's fame and a large part of his happiness in this life depend upon the success of his writings, it is the duty of all his readers to censure him only when they are very sure that they have just grounds for so doing. Irresponsible, uninformed censorious criticism is morally wrong; according to the phrase of Milton it partakes of the nature of spiritual murder. Uninformed enthusiastic praise is also in real-ity unjust to the writer and is certainly unfair to one's fellow men — but this may be passed over as venial. Yet our duty to the writer does not stop here, for we have the posi-tive duty incumbent on us of endeavoring, so far as may be consistent with our other duties in life, to master the general principles of criticism, of reading the current books that the best critics recommend to us, and of trying so to fit ourselves æsthetically, intellectually, and morally that any good writer can make a friend of us when we read his books. This is the golden rule of reading — and it is true, of course, with regard to our attitudes toward all the arts — that we should try to make ourselves the kind of readers we should like to have if we were authors. This does not mean that we should not read for mere recreation, or that the art of literature or any other of the arts should cease to give us pleasure and should yield us only solid benefits; it merely means that in justice to ourselves and to our fellow men who try to please us, we ought to put ourselves into very much such relations with artists as we should sustain with our fellow men in general society. It is our duty to perfect our manners in order to fit ourselves for our social functions; it is similarly our duty, although not so paramount a one, to perfect our judgments and tastes in order to meet half way the artists who seek to minister to our æsthetic pleasures.

There is much in what has just been said

that relates to the duty of the reader to himself. He owes it to himself to do all in his power to put himself into a proper attitude toward the art of literature, simply because it is his duty to try to develop all the faculties that God has given him. Unfortunately such self-training is irksome to most people and thus defeats its own ends; but we may be sure that if we had perfectly balanced souls every step made in the right direction would be pleasurable in itself and would lead to joys ineffable. As it is we are at least under some obligation with regard to the development of our critical faculties; for literature and the arts have their place in every system of liberal education, and we all acknowledge that it is our duty to educate ourselves as well as we can. Hitherto the part played by art in education of a formal character has been so small that we have ignored our responsibilities in the matter; and the fact that the critics have insisted upon pleasure as the end and purpose of art has contributed to the same result. The idea that there is a duty attaching to something that ministers to our pleasures is one that few of us can grasp.

Yet if an art ministers to our spiritual needs — and all true art does — is it not our duty to fit ourselves to appreciate it, and does not appreciation widen and deepen with the training and development of our critical faculties? There can be only one answer to these questions and this answer forces us to acknowledge that the principles of criticism have authority over us all. But what this authority is in kind and degree is and has been for ages a subject of dispute among critics themselves and to investigate the problem in this connection would carry us far beyond the limits of an essay. Besides, I have already discussed the matter to the best of my ability elsewhere in this volume, and it must therefore suffice us here merely to insist that in the interests of self-development the reader must sooner or later submit himself to some sort of critical training and that if we do not at present regard the failure to do this as a moral lapse, it is because we have not yet thought the matter out in all its details, and because we are not yet moral enough as a race in the larger particulars to be able to consider seriously our deficiencies in the smaller particulars.

It is obvious that the duties of the reader toward his fellow men in general cannot be thoroughly separated from his duties toward the writer and toward himself. For example

he owes it to an author who has charmed
him, to acknowledge his debt of gratitude;
but he owes this equally to his fellow men.
One of the most delightful features of sympathetic criticism is its missionary quality. We
cannot rest until we have expatiated to our
friends upon the merits of each fascinating
book we read, and it is not only our privilege
thus to communicate our feelings but our
duty. Yet here as in all missionary work our
responsibilities are great and the need of sub-
mitting ourselves to the authority of criticism
is plain. We have no right to praise unad-
visedly a book or picture. We think that our
individual opinion counts for little, and so it
does, but just as in politics we have no right
to plead our personal insignificance when we
vote carelessly or not at all, so in literary and
artistic matters we have no right to forget that
our individual opinion helps to mould other
opinions and thus to form the popular verdict.
Books become the " book of the hour " more
through the gossip of the club and parlor
than through the praise accorded them by
responsible critical journals. It was gossip
that spread the contagion of Trilby.

But, some one will exclaim, this is refining
and splitting hairs with a vengeance. Life
would not be worth living if one had to weigh

one's praise of a book, a picture, even a magazine article as carefully as one weighs one's words when serving as a witness in an important trial. If a code of artistic ethics like this is to be fastened upon us, the old maxim " Life is short, but art is long " would run for most of us " Life is short, and art is a nuisance."

If there is any justice in this supposed expostulation it lies in the fact that much of what has been said belongs to those " counsels of perfection " that often seem to be counsels of impertinence when we consider how full life is of large moral demands that we cannot satisfy with all our striving and all our prayers. But surely the race would lose ground daily if preachers and teachers and critics and philosophers ceased for one moment to shower " counsels of perfection " upon us. What would Christianity — much more any other religion — become if it were stripped of such counsels?   We may, indeed, make allowances for ourselves and others in all such subtle, scarcely perceptible matters of duty, but we must not the less insist that the sphere of duty is all embracing, that we cannot escape from moral obligations anywhere in this world of ours — not even in the Vatican itself when we stand gazing at one of Raphael's frescoes; for even there our admiration must be mixed with gratitude. Would that all duties were so pleasant!

But if we consent to excuse the average reader from being held to strict account with regard to our "counsels of perfection," we should make no excuse for readers who are clothed with any sort of authority. Even clergymen and lawyers, who are not especially concerned in literature and art, should take care how they pass judgment upon this book and that picture, simply because they are generally looked up to in every community. The teacher — and especially the teacher of literature — occupies a still more responsible position. He forms the mind of youth, and a mere careless word in praise of a book of dubious morality may suffice to give a downward thrust to some young life. His habits of reading, his general attitude toward art are of immense importance in every college community, and indirectly in the world at large. It would be hard to estimate the harm that has been done to the young men of this country through the discovery they must have been making of late that most of their teachers are specialists — knowing only one class of books and caring little for literature and art in their widest application. It would be hard also to estimate the harm done by injudicious methods of presenting the most fascinating subjects that have fallen to the lot of man to teach. But in all these matters there is hope ahead.

We may conclude this branch of our discussion by remarking that there is one great moral obligation resting upon the reader that may be considered in general without reference to our threefold division. It has already been referred to. No reader has a right to expect that an author or an artist shall consult his individual idiosyncrasies, or even his preferences in religious, social, and political matters. We can appreciate a universal art only by cultivating catholicity of spirit. If indeed our mind is made up on this or that important matter, it will follow naturally that the writer or artist who runs counter to our convictions will forfeit that portion of success which is dependent upon his power to give us strictly intellectual pleasure; but if his work of art is great from the point of view of æsthetics and if it yields us the moral pleasure that attaches to what is good in the widest sense, it is a sign of mental inflexibility in us if we fail to receive enjoyment. We simply have no right to let our minds harden to such an extent that they cannot play freely around any work of literary or plastic art. All purely utilitarian demands made upon writers and artists, demands that they shall teach thus and so, that their works shall support our theories — are due to this mental induration from which not one of us escapes. Mr. Hardy's Tess has encountered many such adamantine minds in its short voyage. Whole classes of books sometimes share this fate most undeservedly — as for example the coarse but splendidly powerful novels produced in the last century — particularly those of Fielding. Coarseness and immorality so often go hand in hand that many of us cannot distinguish between them, and our power of isolating ourselves from our own time and civilization is so feeble that our minds cannot play around these books and we express the lurid wish of the late Mr. Sidney Lanier, that they may all be burned *instanter*. The fact is that Fielding's Tom Jones is probably the greatest English novel and that its loss would be a calamity. If, however, experience has proved to us that such books are not good for us, any more than they are for very young minds, it is of course our duty to pass them by. But there is no excuse for our blinking the fact that our minds are indurated or for our setting ourselves up as ultra-pure literary prohibitionists — that is as Pharisees.

IV

IT is clear that nearly everything that has been hitherto said could be made applicable, by means of a few turns of phrase, to our discussion of the relations between the written work and morals in general. It is clear also that the subject might be treated indefinitely; I shall therefore confine myself to one phase of it, to wit, the question how far the moral element in literature seems to have affected the race in its determination of the books it is willing to rank as classics. If any important facts can be obtained with regard to the relations of the classics to morals, it will be far easier to draw inferences with regard to the relations that ought to subsist between morals and general literature than it would be to draw such inferences from purely abstract considerations based on the nature of literature or from a discussion of contemporary phases of literary art. These inferences will not, however, be drawn here, for to draw them would be to protract this essay to a really intolerable length.

The first fact that strikes us in considering the classics from our present point of view is that if we take the absolutely supreme master-pieces of the nations, they are all not merely not immoral, but profoundly and positively moral. The Iliad and the Odyssey, the odes of Pindar and the dramas of Sophocles, the Æneid, the Divine Comedy, the plays of Shakspere, the Don Quixote, the greatest plays of Corneille, Molière, and Racine, the Paradise Lost, Goethe's Faust, the Comédie Humaine, and the Légende des Siècles — all these noble works of genius would be absolutely changed and clearly weakened if we could take from them their capacity to stir our moral emotions. Now could this capacity have existed to such an extent in these masterpieces if their authors had not felt emotions similar to those we experience? It is hard to believe that it could; and it is equally hard to believe that the capability to feel and excite such emotions is not as necessary to a supreme author's success as the more strictly artistic capacity to feel æsthetic emotions and give vent to them by means of infinitely varied rhythm and euphony, and command over the emotional elements of language. The possession and use of the grand style mark off Homer and Dante,

Shakspere and Milton from the mass of poets, but, as Matthew Arnold was never tired of telling us, a " high seriousness " marks them off as well. I am not going to try to defend Mr. Arnold's description of poetry as a " criticism of life " or to take up cudgels in his behalf against the many critics and readers who think that he sometimes mixed disastrously his rôles of critic and moralist; but I will say that I think the whole English speaking world owes him a debt of gratitude for his insistence upon the fact that all really great literature is profoundly moral in tone. It is scarcely necessary to remark that this does not mean that the supreme authors preach to us or that great literature is obtrusively moral or spiritual — outside, of course, of specifically sacred and spiritual books — but it does mean that all of the works belonging to the highest range of the world's classics have their underlying moral basis, just as they have their intellectual basis, and their æsthetic basis.

It is to be observed further that all these works are not merely those that the critics have agreed to rank as supreme, but they are those that the public at large among the respective races and nations that have given them birth have accepted and treated as supreme. The greatest masterpieces of Greek literature, the Iliad and the Odyssey, were also the most popular, and the same is true of the works of Virgil, Dante, Shakspere and Goethe. The Latin race which we are accustomed to regard as not profoundly moral, is in this respect at one with the more sober Teutonic race. The inference is irresistible that no writer can attain the position of a world classic who is not as much an unconscious moralist as he is a conscious or unconscious artist.

Nor is the case altered when we come to consider the great literary men who are either not entitled to rank as supreme classics anywhere or else rank as such only in their own country. Chaucer is an example of the latter class — supreme in English poetry after Shakspere and Milton, he is yet not a world classic. Mr. Arnold has said that this is due to the fact that Chaucer has not sufficient seriousness, and largeness of view. I am inclined to doubt this and to wonder whether Chaucer may not in the more cosmopolitan future attain the rank of a world classic, for it seems to me that he is deeply moral and truly serious under his playful smiles. Be this as it may, Chaucer, even in tales that are coarse to our present notions, is always wholesome and moral and so illustrates the truth of our contention. Spenser with his exquisite purity, illustrates it even better, and so do Gray and Burns. Wordsworth illustrates it, but at the same time shows us that mere seriousness unaccompanied by a continuously great style will not suffice to attain true popularity. Tennyson illustrates admirably how a writer who combines moral seriousness and artistic excellence may attain the summit of contemporary renown. Shelley on the other hand shows us how the possession of exquisite artistic gifts and the warm worship of a zealous body of admirers will not make any writer truly popular if his subject matter be not entirely sound. Even Keats himself is still suffering from the fact that Death did not give him time to ripen the moral side of his nature; and Byron is naturally suffering still more from the same cause. But all these men are true classics because their work, either in whole or in part, will stand the moral test and because it can obviously stand the æsthetic and intellectual tests. Byron indeed has come perilously near falling from the position due to his transcendent genius — there are not wanting people to tell us that he actually has fallen — but here again I find myself by Mr. Arnold's side contending that a large part of his work is sound and that his energy, his sincerity, his humor, his range of intellect and feelings — make him the great literary power that the continental nations still believe him to be.

I have included in the above list of writers none but Englishmen and poets, but I believe that the contention made can easily be established with regard to secondary prose classics in England and with regard to secondary classics generally in the great European literatures. It must be remembered, of course, that as the intellect plays a considerable part in all literature even in poetry, certain writers have attained positions as classics chiefly through the intellectual side of their works. These men are all secondary classics, however, and the moral element is never lacking from their writings, for it is almost impossible to use the intellect in a way that will tell materially upon future generations unless it is used on the side of morals. Pope and Boileau will serve to illustrate the truth of this statement.

The proposition that the supreme and secondary classics of the various nations are on the whole distinctly moral will not, in the natural order of things, escape contradiction. A notorious educator has lately discovered

that Virgil is not a safe author for schoolboys
to read, and Mr. Sidney Lanier's views with
regard to the morality of Fielding and Smol-
lett have just been referred to. I can imagine
quite an army of worthy citizens of the type
of Mr. Comstock brandishing a host of books
at me if I were once to get in their midst and
they were at all widely read. Horace and
Rabelais and Boccaccio and Margaret of
Navarre would shudder to behold their works
used as missiles, and Shakspere would be
almost the only Elizabethan dramatist who
could look on serenely. As to the French
novelists, their only consolation would lie in
the fact that their loosely stitched volumes
would come to pieces so easily as to be in-
effective in offensive warfare. But although
I might be smothered in paper I should die
exclaiming that coarseness is not and never
has been synonymous with immorality and
that no really immoral author has ever won
the suffrages either of the majority of his
contemporaries or of posterity.

This contention has, to be sure, been made
thousands of times ere this, and it will doubtless be made thousands of times hereafter;
but it none the less needs making everywhere
and always. It is the emotions of the author
and the reader that determine the moral

character of a book, and whenever the author has been pure in the main, as has been the case with the truly classical writers, a pure-minded reader of mature years and no special idiosyncrasies will find little or nothing to fault in the morals of the literary work in question. This is true no matter what characters and situations may be found in the book — if it belong to the drama or fiction — or what material in general may be used by the writer. The essential point in all artistic work is the treatment of the materials. Improper materials are those that cannot be treated with pure emotions by any normal artist, hence it is idle to pick out this or that incident from a book and declare that it makes for or against morality unless one can show conclusively that the author has so treated it that normally decent men have their sensibilities shocked by it. This I believe it will be impossible to do with regard to any truly classic book except in the particular of obscenity, which is not immoral *per se* but only by association. If a reader cannot tolerate obscenity he will, as we have already seen, do well to eschew certain noted books, but he should not regard them as necessarily immoral. Such books will probably lose popularity more and more as our tastes change and develop, and they may in the end be practically dropped from the list of the classics unless their positive merits suffice to keep them really alive — but this is a side issue on which enough has been said.

The actually immoral book does not therefore in my opinion stand any chance of ranking among the classics, but it is possible for unmoral books to attain this rank. For example Poe is one of the least positively moral and spiritual authors that I have ever read, but his rank as a classic is indisputable, although part of his comparative lack of success in certain portions of this country may perhaps be traced to the absence of a moral basis for his literary work. But in Poe's case we have a wonderful surplus of æsthetic and intellectual qualities to make up for the deficiency in positively moral qualities. Then again it must be remembered both that his genius moved in spheres so remote from "this dim spot which men call earth" that considerations of morality scarcely seem to apply to his creations, and that there is hardly an author to be named who so little suggests the actually immoral. Poe is an essentially pure writer, yet his purity is so cold and weird that we do not obtain from it the glow needed to excite our moral emotions.

But it is time to bring this essay to an end, and there is perhaps no better way to do this than to sum up briefly the main conclusions suggested by our analysis. We have practically been led to believe that every truly successful author and artist must necessarily possess the emotions of a gentleman, which will ensure the modicum of spirituality required. We have seen further that every reader should strip himself as far as possible of his idiosyncrasies, should meet the author half way, and should exercise due care in forming and uttering his literary opinions. Finally we have found reason to maintain that all truly classic literature has a moral basis, whence we conclude that if the classics continue to exert their due influence we need not fear that immoral and deleterious forms of literature and art can ever really flourish in our midst.[1]

[1] Mr. Justin McCarthy in his delightful Reminiscences (I., 60–64) has lately given us John Bright's interesting theory that all bad characters should be omitted from novels. Perhaps they will be dropped, just as obscenity has been, but the consummation is a good way off.

IV

THE NATURE OF LITERATURE

IV

THE NATURE OF LITERA-
TURE

I

FROM time out of mind critics have endeavored without success to define literature. They have all been more or less able
to describe it; they have all been fairly well
agreed as to many of its chief characteristics; they have seldom failed in the long
run to answer satisfactorily the concrete
question whether a certain piece of writing
belongs or not to literature; and yet they
have never succeeded in discovering infal-
lible tests by which every reader can assure
himself of the literary or non-literary character of any specific composition. In fact,
they have not themselves succeeded in using
the word " literature " with appreciable consistency. The dictionaries, which register
public and critical usage with regard to the
meanings of terms, give us a number of
senses in which this particular term may be

correctly employed. It may be equivalent to "learning;" it may mean "the use of letters for the promulgation of thought or knowledge;" it may signify "recorded thought or knowledge, the aggregate of books and other publications, in either an unlimited or a limited sense"—that is to say, all books, or books in a special language, or about a special subject, such as chemistry; finally, it may express "in a restricted sense the class of writings in which expression and form in connection with ideas of permanent and universal interest are characteristic or essential features, as poetry, romance, history," etc., "in contradistinction to scientific works or those written expressly to impart knowledge."

The above definitions are all taken from the "Century Dictionary," and it will be seen at once that, unless they are analyzed, they will prove of little service to the thoughtful student. The first two uses of the term are plainly of a secondary or derived character, and need not concern us, while we perceive immediately that the third is too large to be of any real value to us. "Recorded thought or knowledge" is a definition that will dignify with the title of literary men the Pharaohs, who carved their names on pyramids; the Roman Emperors, who recorded their exploits on triumphal arches; the Druids, who couched their mysteries in oghams; the English monks, who set down year by year the forays of the Danes; together with the obliging dealers of the present time who compile catalogues of secondhand books, the Congressmen who distribute their own speeches gratis, and the statisticians, expert or otherwise, who superintend the publication of our decennial census. All these enumerated persons, together with mathematicians, chemists, physicians, lawyers, theologians, and the rest of the men who write and print with the result of merely adding to our knowledge, may be worthy of high praise, but cannot be called literary if that epithet is to have any appreciable value. The study of literature under such circumstances would be practically bounded only by the sphere of human knowledge. Some line of demarcation must be drawn if " literature " is to be regarded as anything less than a purely indefinite, almost infinite, term.

Such a line of demarcation has been drawn in the framing of the fourth definition given above, and it coincides obviously with that adopted by De Quincey when he wrote of the literature of knowledge as opposed to the literature of power, as well as with that chosen by Charles Lamb when he distinguished between books that are "no books" and books that are really books—which live and delight their readers—the kind of books Milton had in mind when he wrote that it would be as wicked to kill a good book as to kill a good man. Mr. John Morley also gives the same idea in a slightly different form when he says that "literature consists of all the books—and they are not so many—where moral truth and human passion are touched with a certain largeness, severity, and attractiveness of form."

But have we not passed from too large a definition of our term to one that is too small? Are not some of Mr. Huxley's essays, which he intended to make and did make scientific in character, regarded as literature by many people, and on just grounds? Again, are the *ideas* expressed by such a poem as Poe's Ulalume fairly to be described as possessing permanent and universal interest, or does the poem itself touch *moral truth* with any *largeness* of form? Yet are we prepared to say that Ulalume is not literature, even though it is not a

book, and is thus outside the precise terms
of Mr. Morley's definition?

The truth is that, while we are plainly on
the right track when we attempt to separate
the nobly moving and powerful books from
those that merely convey information in a
more or less perfunctory manner, we find it
difficult to get a definition that will suit us,
because we are trying to define what is really
the product of an art, and may therefore be,
so far as its subject-matter is concerned,
as large as life expressed in terms of the
medium of expression peculiar to that art
can ever be. Now life itself is practically
indefinable and infinite, and, as one can
recognize almost at a glance, the medium of
expression used by the art of literature —
to wit, words in certain combinations — is
practically infinite also. We are, therefore,
trying to define a product that may assume
as many forms almost as life — an attempt
which is hopeless, especially when we insist
on laying stress upon subject-matter in
framing our definition. We simply cannot
say that literature is in essence any particular thing, because its subject-matter, which
is its essence, may be everything. But we
may perhaps find it possible to get a working description of literature that will suffice

for all our purposes if we will frankly say
that we believe that there is such a thing as
an art of literature which expresses itself
by means of words, much as music does
by means of sounds, painting by means of
an arrangement of colors on some material,
etc. Then, without asking ourselves what
our finished literary product is in its essence,
let us ask ourselves what methods of employing words have been used by great
writers in the past to produce work which
the world has agreed to regard as literary
in character. In other words, we will imitate
the critic of music who studies to determine
the artistic methods of the great composers
of recent times. If we can find that there
are certain principles of word-arrangement
common to all works that the world has received as good literature, just as there are
certain principles of sound-arrangement common to all true music, we shall then be able
to say with confidence that literature is the
product of an art which deals with words in
a certain way; and if our "certain way"
be not easily definable, we need not be surprised, for all art is the expression of human
genius, which is itself indefinable, and many
things in this life can be recognized that cannot be defined.

It must be admitted, of course, that, in treating literature as the sum total of the products of what we have called literary art, we are not improving our condition from the point of view of critical theory. It is much easier to describe any art than to define it, but students of painting and the other fine arts have usually less difficulty than students of literature in describing the products of their respective arts. This is mainly because they begin with certain freely conceded postulates with regard to the nature of art in general. They assume that the product of any art must, to be legitimate, give pleasure of an emotional kind connected with the idea of beauty, although, according to some critics, pleasure of an intellectual kind connected with the idea of truth and of a moral kind connected with the idea of right conduct, are often present also, and in the greatest works of art are indispensable.[1] They assume, further, that when the quality of usefulness is connected with a work of art, it must not interfere considerably with the quality of beauty. Making the satisfaction of the æs-

[1] Here and elsewhere I make no pretence of using psychological terms with scientific accuracy. I trust, however, that the untechnical terms employed will make my meaning sufficiently clear.

thetic sense a *sine qua non* of artistic production, art critics are thus, on the whole, able to pronounce with adequate certainty on the question whether a given product is artistic or not, because they ask rather what a work of art does, than what it is in its essence. They ask also what the artist does, consciously or unconsciously, in order to make a work of art produce its legitimate pleasurable effect upon the æsthetic sense. Thus, as a rule, they continually avoid metaphysical questions — although these have their interest — and deal with more or less concrete phases of their subject.

Let us now apply their methods to what we call literary art, and see whether we shall not obtain more tangible results than we should do were we to continue to endeavor to define literature. We may, indeed, find before we have finished that literature is a rather complex art, consisting of poetry which corresponds with music and painting and sculpture, in which the elements of use and often of moral and intellectual emotion play a decidedly inferior part to the element of æsthetic emotion, and prose which holds partly by the arts named above, and partly by architecture, in which the element of use enters conspicuously. The complex character of our art need not, however, render our method of treatment particularly difficult or in any way unserviceable, nor need the fact that intellectual and moral emotions of a pleasurable, kind often predominate over æsthetic emotions in prose and, for some minds, even in poetry, hinder us from regarding literature as the product of an art, since the *sine qua non* of all art — viz., an appeal to the æsthetic sense — will be found to exist in all literature that good critics have been agreed in considering worthy of attention, and since the element of pleasure, on the part both of creator and of recipient, continually abides.

II

IN pursuance of our plan of treatment let us now examine the following statement, which has resulted from a considerable analysis of the problem we have just been discussing, and see if it will help us appreciably: In order to produce literature or to practise the art of literature a writer must record not merely his thought or his knowledge or both, but also express his sustained æsthetic, intellectual, and moral emotions in such a way as to awaken in a sustained manner similar emotions in others.

We shall do well to explain by means of an example. An important historical event happens — a fictitious event would serve our purpose just as well — and a man knowing the facts about it writes them down. This man, no matter who he may be, even a mediæval monk, will probably have emotions, æsthetic, intellectual, and moral, connected with the event he records; but unless he has the power, conscious or unconscious, to give these emotions expression in his record, what he writes will not be literature in any true sense. He will not write history, but annals of an unliterary kind. Yet this man, though he may not be capable of an original thought, may, nevertheless, if he has power to fuse his knowledge and accompanying emotions, produce something that is truly literary in character. He does not write history as yet, but he does write picturesque and entertaining annals. If now to knowledge and emotions he adds thought, if he traces effects to their causes and draws conclusions, if his thought be truly original and philosophical, he has done all that he can do in a literary way for the actual event, he has written history in its highest and truest sense. If, however, our hypothetical writer, with his abundant knowledge and his philosophical powers of thought, had been either capable of no emotions, an improbable supposition, or destitute of the power of expressing them, he would most certainly not have produced a literary work. He would, perhaps, have made a contribution to the philosophy of history, but not to history in the sense in which the student of literature applies that noble term. Furthermore, if our writer's emotions, or his power of expressing them, had been merely momentary or intermittent, and not fairly sustained, he would have written something that could not, as a whole, have been called literature, in spite of the fact that literary fragments might have been embedded in it. The same thing is true when several writers of varying powers join to produce a common work, as for example the Anglo-Saxon Chronicle, which contains literature, but is not itself, as a whole, literature at all.

Finally, our would-be historian or picturesque annalist must possess not merely adequate knowledge, with or without original thought, and emotions which he can express so as to relieve his tension of soul; he must possess also the power of so expressing his emotions as to make others feel them. A sustained and, so to speak, contagious expression of emotion, which must be partly æsthetic in character, is the indispensable condition to every piece of writing that has any claims to be considered as literature, if literature be regarded as the product of an art. It sometimes happens that a man possessing adequate knowledge, original thought, and vivid emotions, which are not correlated by that faculty, of which we shall speak hereafter, known as the imagination, expresses himself in a way presumably sufficient to relieve his own pent-up feelings, but not in a way capable of appreciably communicating these feelings to others.[1] Such a man, we say, lacks literary or, as some would put it, stylistic or imaginative capacity, and as a consequence his book, if it survive at all, lives only for special students. Under these circumstances we are immediately led to ask (putting aside the consideration of those writers who deal chiefly with thought and emotion apart from external knowledge — that is, philosophers of a literary turn) if there

[1] It is probably by some such reasoning that we must explain the existence among us of a large number of would-be authors who are unsuccessful in spite of many good qualities of mind and heart.

is any medium of expression by the use of which a writer of ability can always relieve his own surcharged emotions, and at the same time surely communicate them to others.

There must be such a medium of expression, or literature in our sense of the term cannot exist; for, as we have seen, the sustained and contagious expression of emotion is what serves to distinguish the writings of the mere knower and thinker from those of the literary man or artist proper. We cannot say that the possession and use of such a medium of expression is the sole requisite of the true man of letters, for a modicum of thought and, in a sense, of knowledge also, or what we may term a " carrying statement " is necessary to every literary work, since the power of expressing emotion pure and simple is assigned to the other fine arts like music and painting, which cannot present thought at all, but only suggestions to thought. Yet it is perfectly true to say that with the possession and use of a highly developed medium for the expression and communication of his emotions a writer can produce vital literature almost without thinking a tangible thought or recording a thing worth knowing. Poe's Ulalume is a striking proof of the truth of this statement. But it is time to endeavor to determine what our desiderated medium of expression is in its essence.[1]

[1] It has been assumed throughout the above discussion that the artist consciously or unconsciously communicates his emotions to us through the medium of his art product; but this assumption will not win full assent until we examine what is meant by a phrase constantly used by critics — to wit, "impersonal art." Perhaps some citations from Mr. Bernhard Berenson will enable us to indicate the nature of the problem. "Velasquez, who painted without ever betraying an emotion," is the first; the second is longer and runs as follows: "If a given situation in life, a certain aspect of landscape, produces an impression upon the artist, what must he do to make us feel it as he felt it? There is one thing he must not do, and that is to reproduce his own feeling about it. That may or may not be interesting, may or may not be artistic; but one thing it certainly cannot do, it cannot produce upon us the effect of the original situation in life or the original aspect of the landscape; for the feeling is not the original phenomenon itself, but the phenomenon, to say the least, as refracted by the personality of the artist, and this personal feeling, being another thing, must needs produce another effect." (The Central Italian Painters of the Renaissance, pp. 70, 71.)

We may note that there is nothing here that interferes with the idea that the artist experiences emotions in connection with some external phenomenon, which emotions he wishes us to realize. We note, further, that no question is raised with regard to subjective art proper, such as that of the lyric poet whose feeling is often the real thing to be described rather than the external phenomenon that has occasioned the feeling. The whole question is plainly one of method. Mr. Berenson holds that the great artist will strive to avoid the effects of the "personal equation," much as a scientist will, and in the highest ranges of objective art this is true. The dramas of Shakspere, for exam-

III

THAT it consists primarily of words goes
without saying.   Thought and knowledge, if
ple, are in the main impersonal.   But while it is correct,
from one point of view, to affirm that Velasquez painted
and Shakspere wrote without betraying an emotion, it is
hardly correct to say that either painted or wrote without
more or less consciously intending to communicate to
others certain emotional states which the mere reproduction of the external phenomenon could not be relied on to
convey.   Mere reproduction is photography, and neither
Velasquez nor Shakspere was a photographer.   Certain
emotional states, such as those of exaltation, of admiration, of contempt, must, it would seem, actually characterize the artist while he is producing.   He cannot be a
mere lens; he must be inspired.   But when he is inspired
he is out of himself, and hence is impersonal, although
really in a state of exaltation which he is trying to reproduce in us.   He is not conscious, perhaps, of his endeavor,
certainly not in a personal and selfish way; but for the
convenience of our analysis we may assume that what he
does is actually to try to make us feel something.   He
would not paint or write if this were not his motive, yet
he may have this motive and be as much out of himself as
a thoroughly spiritual man is when he performs some act
of heroic self-abnegation.   But the experience of sustained
emotions and the inspired, unselfish impulse to stir such
emotions in others in connection with the exciting phenomenon seem to be the basal facts in all art creation; and
if the artist really paints or writes without betraying an
emotion, it is because he is great enough to prevent his
brush or pen from expressing any single characteristically
personal emotion which he perceives would introduce a

they are to serve any definite purpose, must be presented to us in more or less con-

disturbing element of self, a result which experience has told him would be dangerous; or else it is because he is in that condition of creative exaltation which the Greeks attributed to their poets and which Matthew Arnold had in mind when he said that it seemed as if Nature sometimes took the pen out of Wordsworth's hand and wrote for him. We may rest assured, therefore, that the theory of the emotional basis of all art and of the communication of the artist's emotions to spectator or reader is not really affected by anything that can be said about the nature and value of impersonal art. Emotions, or at least an emotional state, can be communicated in an impersonal, unconscious way in art as well as in conduct. We may conclude this lengthy side discussion by a brief consideration of what ought to be the most impersonal of all art attitudes, if we may so speak : that of the portrait-painter. Here the artist should surely strive to reproduce the sitter in the most faithful way on canvas ; in other words, he ought not to let us suspect the existence of the "personal equation." But it is hard to believe that if the sitter excited a state of emotional contempt in the artist this contempt would not inevitably be communicated through the picture to the beholder. So a great painter having a hero to paint for whom he felt admiration would almost inevitably transmit that admiration. Friendship, indifference, every emotional state, seems to get itself transferred to canvas; or else, if these moral emotions are absent, there are æsthetic emotions connected with movement and what the critics call "tactile values" which in the main occupy the artist and are transmitted to us. Perhaps the best portraits, technically speaking, are those in which æsthetic emotions like these have dominated the artist, but it is hard for some of us to feel that in the case of the noble portraits by Raphael to be seen in the great Florentine double gallery there was nected wholes, and this is done among all civilized peoples only through the use of words, spoken or written. The emotions of the man who seeks literary utterance must, as we have seen, attach themselves to at least a modicum of thought and knowledge, to a carrying statement; hence these emotions, to have literary value, must be expressed in words. A series of twenty piercing cries would express profound emotion, but would not be in the least sense literary in character.[1] Our medium, then, must consist of words spoken or written. But for all practical purposes literature must be something recorded, something preserved, that can be enjoyed and re-enjoyed. Before the days of writing and printing literature was remembered, not recorded; but nowadays we record, and do not try to remember. The spoken word practically perishes, therefore, and need not be considered as literature in any strict sense, since the phonograph has not been yet put to serious use. Hence orators

not some strong moral emotion continually affecting the earnest painter as he toiled away upon his task of giving life to his canvases and pleasure tempered with moral awe to us who now behold his handiwork.

[1] Such a series might be used in a piece of literature with considerable effect. I have an impression that one is to be found in the Philoctetes.

whose words are not reported, which is
naturally rare at present, are literary men who
do not produce literature. Our medium consists, therefore, of recorded words, and nowadays of written or printed words couched in
alphabetical symbols. Literature might, of
course, be presented in symbols other than
alphabetical, but this fact does not affect our
analysis. These recorded or — let us say
hereafter — *written* words, as they must convey a modicum of thought and knowledge, a
carrying statement, should be arranged according to the laws of syntax, and, indeed, in
order that they may produce a uniform and
ascertainable impression, should be used in
accordance with all the normal laws of grammar and rhetoric, so far as the latter study is
concerned with intelligibility, unless, indeed,
we wish to produce certain legitimate effects
of illusion through the use of an illiterate
dialect. This is but to say that our words
should be grouped properly into phrases,
clauses, sentences, and paragraphs; that
grammar and rhetoric are sciences that un-
derlie literature. There is also another underlying science — viz., logic. It is plain that
our words grammatically and rhetorically
grouped, since they are to convey thought
and knowledge, cannot make obvious non-

sense. If in any way they cause the mind to go through reasoning processes, they should guide correctly, and not perplex or nonplus the reader's intellect. On the same principle our grouped words must be true to all such facts of experience as are essential to the validity of the thought and knowledge to be conveyed. Such a group of words as " giant scrub oaks " could be admitted into a literary work only when some special reason, such as an attempt at humor, justified the combination.

We see, then, that our written words must be arranged and governed in the manner indicated above; in other terms, our medium of expression must consist of written words that are not incongruous. It is at once obvious that such words ought to be sufficient to convey all the thought and knowledge that we can ever have to express under normal circumstances. We need only inquire, therefore, how written words that make sense can be made to receive sustained emotions of a pleasurable sort, and to communicate them to the reader. This can be accomplished first by imparting to one's words adequate rhythm and euphony and harmony; secondly, by using in addition words that connote things and ideas, the suggestion of which will call up in the reader emotions which are not strained, and in which the element of pleasure on the whole predominates over that of pain. It follows, if what has just been stated be true, that our medium of expression must consist of written words specially chosen and specially arranged, and that the essential problem before every would-be literary man, after he has mastered the rules of grammar, of rhetoric, so far as they relate to intelligibility, and of logic, and has obtained sufficient thought and knowledge to serve as a basis or a carrying statement for the emotions he would impart, is concerned with the choice of emotive words and their rhythmical, euphonious, and harmonious arrangement. The more valuable the thought and knowledge he can contrive to convey with these emotive and attractively arranged words the more important in all cases his literary work will be; but he is none the less primarily concerned with the choice and arrangement of words — that is to say, he must, consciously or unconsciously, apply all the principles of rhetoric, including poetics, that do not relate specifically to mere intelligibility. Now let us endeavor to obtain some adequate information upon these important matters of the arrangement and the choice of written words necessary to the production of real literature.

IV

WORDS in a truly literary composition are arranged rhythmically because, as psychology teaches us, it is a law of our nature for our emotions to express themselves rhythmically and to be excited by rhythm. Rhythm, from a Greek word that means " flowing," is " movement in time characterized by equality of measures and by alternation of tension (stress) and relaxation." It is represented in nature by the beating of the heart, by the movement of waves, by the swaying of leaves. In speech it is represented by the succession of emphatic and unemphatic syllables, which delights the ear just as the rhythmical sway-ing of a blade of grass delights the eye. There is, of course, some sort of rhythm in all speech — a fact which unites this noble capacity of man with the universal life of nature — for all life seems to be based on motion, in which rhythm could invariably be discovered if we only had the proper organs of apprehension. But the rhythm latent in conversation and in the written style — writ-ten words sounded to the *inner* ear yield rhythm — of men who have no great power of translating their emotions into language is practically unrecognizable for the most part; hence it is that conversation, unless it concern some exciting topic, pleasant or unpleasant, or be conducted by a master of the art, fails, as a rule, to appeal profoundly to our emotions, and the same is true of the majority of the books that are written. When, however, the emotions of an author are really excited, he tends to arrange his words in such a way that they either suggest a rhythm that stimulates the emotions of others or else fall into an unmistakable rhythm which can be measured accurately. In the former case he composes what we call normally literary prose; in the latter case he composes something in measured rhythm, or metre, which we call usually poetry. These two divisions exhaust literature between them.[1]

[1] There is no need to discuss at any length the time-worn question whether there can be such a thing as poetry not couched in metrical language. According to the terms of our description of literature, all the essential features of literary production will be found in every piece of true prose and verse; the line of demarcation furnished by measurement of rhythm is, therefore, essential only in the determination of questions relative to degree of emotional pleasure excited, not to kind. It seems to be clear, from the data of general experience, that the emotional pleasure resulting from the use of measured rhythm is, all other things being equal, and the subject or carrying statement

Now it is obvious that while there is a specific line of demarcation — viz., the possibility of measurement of rhythm — between literary prose and poetry, there is none, so far as rhythm is concerned, between literary prose and prose that is not literary. But the absence of a line of strict demarcation proves no more in this case than it does in the case of the animal and vegetable kingdoms. There are forms of life, like sponges, that seem or once seemed to belong to either kingdom or to both; so there are kinds of prose about which it might be impossible to decide fully whether they belong to the category of literary prose or not. But above and below sponges we get unmistakable animals and plants, and so above and below the dubious varieties of prose mentioned we get prose that is plainly literary and the reverse — the assumption being made, of course, that with the majority of educated readers,

being capable of sustaining the more intense emotional force resulting from the use of measured rhythm, greater than that consequent upon the employment of unmeasured rhythm; hence it is advisable to insist firmly on the fact that there is a literature couched in measured rhythm which we call by convention poetry, and a literature couched in unmeasured rhythm which we call by convention prose. The names are thus seen to be conventional, but the varieties of literature that they represent are distinct in one important particular. See note 1, page 170.

or else with the body of critics, the power resides of speaking more or less authoritatively on such points. If now what has just been said be true, it follows that literature in prose must be characterized by an adequate rhythm. The amount and character of this rhythm need not occupy us here, although it should be noted that some critics have denied that rhythm is necessary to literary prose. What does concern us is simply the fact that rhythm, being the language of the emotions, is naturally employed in literature, the chief purpose of which is to embody these, and that, therefore, our would-be writer of literature must consciously or unconsciously employ rhythm whether he write in prose or verse.

With regard to the euphonious arrangement of words, it may be observed that this, while not of such prime necessity as rhythmic arrangement, is nevertheless necessary in a secondary sense to all real literature, whether prose or poetry. Euphony, which is Greek for " having a good voice," implies a distinctly pleasant arrangement of sounds in composition, and when we say that words in true literature should be arranged euphoniously we mean merely that care should be taken not to let the combination of sounds made by the words we use offend the outer or the inner ear by their dissonance or frequent repetition. The waves caused by certain combinations of sounds produce physical effects upon the auditory nerves that are translated into unpleasant emotions on the part of the reader — for example, this effect is produced by an undue succession of s's as well as by the monotonous repetition of single words, phrases, or clauses, the sound or sound-combinations of which might not have been unpleasant when experienced singly. But unpleasant feelings or emotions on the part of the reader obviously interfere with the transmission to him of the pleasant emotions of which the literary product is intended to be the medium. Hence the necessity of a euphonious arrangement of words is apparent.

With regard to the necessity of a harmonious arrangement of words we can afford to be equally brief. Harmony, strictly speaking, refers to the adaptation of sound to sense, and is not required by the ear to anything like the same extent as rhythm and euphony. Still it has at times a distinct part to play in affecting the emotions of a reader, and is more or less to be found in all good literary work. And akin to harmony in sound is what we may call a mental harmony that should attach to a truly literary arrangement of words. It cannot be doubted that there is a mental pleasure that results from the harmonious, or perhaps it would be best to say symmetrical, arrangement of the words and combinations of words that we employ which is analogous to the pleasure the eye obtains from the contemplation of symmetry in figures. A felicitous balanced or periodic sentence carries with it a charm of symmetry that gives pleasure to the cultivated and often to the uncultivated reader, and so enhances the emotive value of the writing in which it is found. It cannot be doubted, also, that the attainment of symmetry in our arrangement of words often enhances their euphony in a subtle manner and helps us to attain that adequate rhythm which is necessary to literary prose. Aristotle long ago pointed out that the period gave a sort of framework to the rhythm, helping it, probably, much as the blank verse period helps that subtle metre, but we need not enlarge on this here. It is sufficient for us to perceive in a general way why a rhythmical, euphonious, harmonious, and, we may add perhaps, symmetrical arrangement of words is a natural medium for the expression and communication of emotions.

V

WE come now to the second of our methods for enabling written words to convey emotion — to wit, the choice of such words as connote an adequate number of ideas and things, the suggestion of which will call up in the reader emotions which are not over-tense and in which the element of pleasure predominates on the whole over that of pain.[1] It might seem at first sight as if such choice of emotive words would be of itself sufficient

[1] It is obvious that pleasure must predominate over pain in the emotive effects of a work of art, or the latter would fail to accomplish the purpose for which all the arts exist. Even where the object represented is in itself one that, if fully realized in actual life, would cause us intensely painful emotions, thoroughly artistic representation will give us emotions on the whole pleasurable. This truth is illustrated in tragedy where the individual pity and fear of the spectator are made universalized emotions through the art of the poet, and are thus purged of grosser elements, with the result that the sympathetic nature receives an emotional relief that is distinctly pleasing. (See with regard to this " purging " the Κάθαρσις of Aristotle, Butcher's Aristotle's Theory of Poetry and the Fine Arts, page 225.) Sometimes what would be unpleasantly disgusting in actual life receives in art a representation that is humorous and provokes pleasant smiles, as is illustrated by a well-known picture by Rubens in the Uffizi gallery.

to express and convey emotions, and so to constitute literature, that literature is after all, merely a matter of diction. A moment's reflection will enable us, however, to see that this is not so, since rhythm is in some way essential to the utterance of emotions and, if not adequately present, is missed with the result that the composition is partly displeasing, and since lack of euphony and harmony would in almost every case take away so much from the effects of the emotive terms used that the reader would experience sensations the reverse of pleasing. On the other hand, it is possible for words rhythmically, euphoniously, and harmoniously arranged to give pleasure without the presence of a single recognizably emotive word — a pleasure sufficient perhaps to assure a reader that he is perusing something that belongs to literature. This can be proved by showing a person ignorant of Latin how to read aloud properly some of Virgil's lines. He will in most cases feel delighted with what he does not understand, and will be ready to admit that it must possess high literary value, and this quite apart from the pleasant effect produced, as we shall see, by the vague.[1] It

---

[1] It is dubious whether doggerel in a foreign language, read naturally, would produce this effect, for the simple

may be doubted, however, whether, strictly speaking, any writer has ever put together a considerable number of words in a really rhythmical, euphonious, and harmonious manner without employing emotive terms.

But whether or not emotive words are always present in any given piece of truly literary work, it is easy to see why their use is more or less necessary. There are many things and ideas about which we have emotions stored up. The words that represent these things and ideas act very much as the electric spark that discharges a heap of powder. The moment we hear them, our stored-up emotions explode, as it were, and we are aglow with delight. For example, in the splendid lines of Keats,

> Charmed magic casements opening on the foam
> Of perilous seas in faery-lands forlorn,

reason that doggerel does not carry emotion with it, and when read aloud to a person ignorant of the language would not be likely to affect him pleasantly unless the reader threw unwarranted emotion into his reading. We may notice in this connection that doggerel does not come under our description of literature, and thus is not poetry, although it is couched in metre, either because it contains no emotive words, as in the mnemonic jingle, "Thirty days hath September," or because such emotive words and their metrical setting as are used in it are in some way incongruous or commonplace.

every epithet and practically all the nouns
will be found to call up emotions. Think
of what emotions, dating back to our childhood, the word " faery-lands " unlocks!
Even the unusual spelling has an emotional
value. There is almost no limit to the emotive power of properly chosen and arranged
words; indeed, a mere word itself that is
unfamiliar and euphonious will often produce emotions which former experience of
the vague and uncertain has stored up in us.
For instance, Milton's line,

Looks toward *Namancos* and *Bayona's* hold,

has caused special emotions of pleasure to
many people chiefly because they knew
nothing about the two small places in Spain
which have been identified only of recent
years by zealous commentators. On the
other hand, it should be remarked that a
new word, not suggestive of the vague and
not specially euphonious, calls up naturally
little or no emotion — which is a partial ex-
planation of the fact that as our vocabulary
improves so does our literary appreciation.

But we have perhaps said enough about
the value of the use of emotive words in
literature, and it remains only to explain
our qualifying remarks about the necessity

of avoiding a strain to the reader's emotions
and a predominance of pain over pleasure.
Our qualification is dependent, of course,
on the fact that literature in our sense of
the term is one of the fine arts, and that,
as we have seen, one of the main objects
of all the fine arts is to give pleasure.
We are secure of pleasure, to a certain
extent, if the words presented to us are
rhythmically, euphoniously, and harmoniously arranged, but so great is the emotive
force of words that it may happen that the
mysterious inner self, which underlies our
emotions, may be overstirred or strained by
the discharge of too powerful or of painful
emotions previously stored up, and that in
consequence the pleasure resulting from the
perception of rhythm, euphony, and harmony may be neutralized by pain caused
by overstressed or unsuitable emotions, or
actually drowned therein. It is just here
that many writers, even experienced ones,
are liable to go astray. They use a word
which to them connotes pleasure, and find
to their surprise that it connotes for another
only what is disagreeable. They use a combination of words that leaves a sense of
delicate sweetness with them and with some
of their friends, and behold! the general

public has only the sense of being cloyed and of wonder at the number of minor poets continually being discovered by enthusiastically generous critics.

VI

BUT this power which we posit of using emotive words that kindle emotions in the reader, what is it but another way of naming that faculty which by some critics under the influence of the Germans and of Coleridge is held to impart the determining characteristic of all truly literary products — the faculty of the creative imagination? The poet or prose writer who possesses imagination transforms the empirical world into an ideal world of images, and in the process finds what we term his æsthetic emotions pleasurably excited. His intellectual and moral emotions, to use our former phraseology, are also sympathetically affected and cannot be satisfied (certainly in the case of the moral ones) without some effort on his part to communicate them to other people. He makes use at once of the medium of expression most suitable to his purpose — viz., words rhythmically, euphoniously, and harmoniously arranged, his æsthetic sense directing him as to the most fitting rhythm and sound-sequences that he can employ. This same sense or, if we prefer so to term it, his imagination teaches him also what words have most power to express the emotions with which he is surcharged. These emotions are the result of his transformation of the actual world of experience into an ideal world of images, and the faculty which enabled him to form mental images enables him also to find emotive words which will call up such images in the minds of all who read him, provided they too are gifted with imagination, not indeed necessarily creative, but at least receptive. Hence it is that in all highly emotive literature, such as poetry and oratory, the words used tend, either singly or in combination, to be representative of concrete images, or at least to suggest such images vividly — which is but to say that figurative language is essential to highly emotive literature. We see, therefore, that our preceding analysis of the nature of the medium of expression employed in the production of literature might be resumed in the single statement that literature consists of words chosen and arranged by the imaginative faculty.

There is, however, one other point to be considered before we can regard our analysis as fairly complete. Properly chosen and arranged emotive words will give us literary pleasure from the moment we begin a good poem or piece of prose, but an additional pleasure comes to us as we progress in our reading and become conscious of the symmetry of the parts of the composition and, finally, of its unity as a whole. These emotions, connected with symmetry and unity, are very complex, and seem to be partly æsthetic, partly intellectual, partly moral in character. The perception of symmetry, so far as the quality does not affect the rhythm, harmony, and euphony of the composition, can hardly be æsthetic, but is rather intellectual in character, since neither the eye nor the ear, the two channels through which excitations to æsthetic pleasure are in the main received from the outer world, is affected, but only the mind. The perception of unity gives an unmistakable intellectual pleasure, but this seems to disappear when the whole that is imaged by the imaginative composition — whether it be an action or a character or some feature of external nature that is portrayed — is realized completely for what it is. Then, according as our sense for beauty or our sense for conduct is stirred, the pleasure consequent upon the perception of unity — that is, the intellectual emotion, merges into an æsthetic or a moral emotion, or, perhaps, into a mixed one, if such a thing be possible.[1] If the intellectual pleasure resulting from the perception of unity be thus lost in the æsthetic pleasure indicated above, it follows that the æsthetic emotions which, according to our analysis, are unloosed by the reading of a truly literary composition are supplemented by a varying quantity of similar emotions which serve to crown our reading with complete success,[2] and which may, when they have somewhat cooled, excite into sympathetic action moral emotions of gratitude to

[1] This merging of one emotion into another is sometimes accomplished so quickly as to escape observation, but perhaps takes place whenever we are brought in contact with any work of art. For example, in contemplating a fine flower piece we probably have an instantaneous perception of the unity of the composition, with a resulting intellectual pleasure which passes into an æsthetic pleasure consequent upon imaginative contact with something that delights the eye, and which may become powerful once more when we have gazed sufficiently.

[2] It is probably this concluding stock of emotions that is chiefly revitalized when we remember books with pleasure.

the literary artist who has charmed us and of thankfulness to the Divine Power that has bestowed the gift of creative imagination upon our fellow man and of receptive imagination upon ourselves. Moral emotions of a similar kind are excited also by the intellectual emotions that come to us during our perusal of a work of literature through our perception of symmetry in the parts of the composition. It must be remembered, however, that intellectual and moral emotions connected with the perception of symmetry and unity may be excited in us by works not at all literary in character; as, for example, by a process of mathematical or scientific reasoning. Hence we infer that the only safe test for determining whether a given product is literary or not is to ascertain whether or not it affects pleasurably the æsthetic sense.[1]

[1] We must refrain, for lack of space, from discussing Schopenhauer's suggestive essay on Beauty and Interest in Works of Art further than to say that if we agree with him in regarding "beauty as an affair of knowledge" that appeals to the knowing subject because it is always connected with the *idea*, while interest, on the other hand, is an affair of the *will*, we may nevertheless contend that the idea of beauty is inseparably connected with emotions to which we give the name "æsthetic," while interest is connected with emotions either of intellectual curiosity or of moral sympathy or repulsion. The value of our analysis remains, therefore, unaffected by Schopenhauer's ingeni-

We have now practically obtained the description of literature that we set out to seek, and we perceive that each one of its component terms may be made a test to determine by its presence or absence whether a given product is literature or not. We have found that nothing belongs to real literature unless it consists of written words that constitute a carrying statement which makes sense, arranged rhythmically, euphoniously, and harmoniously, and so chosen as to connote an adequate number of ideas and things the suggestion of which will call up in the reader sustained emotions which do not produce undue tension and in which the element of pleasure predominates, on the whole, over that of pain. Practically every term of this description should be kept in our minds, so that we may consciously apply it as a test to any piece of writing about the literary character of which we are in doubt. It now behooves us to endeavor to determine what consequences will naturally flow from the

ous discussion, nor is it affected by the subtle speculations of Vernon Lee and C. Anstruther Thompson in their recent articles in the Contemporary Review entitled Beauty and Ugliness, articles which, whether accepted in their entirety or not, make a most important contribution to that theory of æsthetics which British and American critics so thoroughly neglect, to the detriment of their work.

stand we have taken with regard to this vexed question of the nature of literature.

VII

ONE or two consequences have been already noted. We have of course set outside the pale of literature all speech that is not recorded, and we have treated similarly all the records of mere knowledge or of thought or of both. We have insisted on the presence of sustained æsthetic emotions in the writer, which are so expressed as to appeal in a sustained and pleasurable manner to the æsthetic sense of the reader. This is but to say that we have insisted that all true literature must move us in a personal way, which may be intellectual and moral in character, but must also be æsthetic. It follows, then, that our description of literature will transsect many of the received categories of prose; for all true poetry, appealing as it does to the æsthetic emotions, is plainly literature by the terms of our analysis. For example, we infer that there are biographies which are mere material for the historical specialist, such as those family memoirs so popular at present, and biographies that belong to permanent literature, like Boswell's Johnson. Books of travel, of history, and of criticism may be similarly divided. The moment we refuse to be guided by subject-matter, the moment we ask primarily what a book does rather than what it is, we find that the number of books contained in many of the categories of prose shrivels considerably.

It is, however, only the categories that do not lend themselves especially to emotional exploitation that so shrink. Whenever a category of prose like the novel naturally holds by the emotions we find that our tests are really more liberal than those applied by most critics. We ask only that the composition to be judged shall consist of words sufficiently well chosen and arranged to produce a sustained and pleasurable effect upon the æsthetic sense, positing always, of course, that the composition in question shall conform to the laws of grammar and logic, and shall be so far true to nature and experience as not to produce intellectual dissatisfaction sufficient to neutralize the desiderated æsthetic excitation.[1]

---

[1] It is just here, of course, that most writers of fiction fail to satisfy the demands of readers of wide experience and culture, while pleasing the masses who are without high or strict standards.

It will be observed that we here ask only for certain positive qualities of feeling and style, and for not much positive thought or intellectual power, pure and simple, and that not a few novelists could stand our tests; whereas, very few, considering the vast number that write, stand the tests applied by most critics and historians of literature. This leads us to consider a very important question. Are not our tests really too easy? Must we not require, besides emotion, a considerable amount of positive intellectual power in every writer whose work is worthy to be called literary? We have already forestalled these questions, and partly answered them, by citing the case of Poe's Ulalume, and we might fortify ourselves by quoting much from M. Victor Hugo, whom some of us regard as the greatest poet since Goethe, and from Hugo's English admirer, Mr. Swinburne. None of these poets has ever produced anything that is not literary in a very real and sometimes a very high sense; but they have all been capable of writing a good deal of undoubted poetry that required very little exercise of the strictly intellectual powers for its production. Our illustrations might be greatly extended, more particularly of course in the field of poetry, where pure emotion can sustain itself better than in prose without what we may call intellectual vitalizing; but we have said enough for our purpose. We have not, however, commented sufficiently on the classes of persons by whom our tests should be applied, and when we shall have done this, it will appear at a glance that we have really obtained elastic, rather than easy, methods of determining what literature is in its essence.

It will be obvious enough to any one who has followed our reasoning closely, that when we demand that all compositions which consist of words so chosen and arranged as to excite sustained and pleasurable æsthetic emotions shall be denominated literature, we must either posit some typical reader whose æsthetic sense will serve as a standard, or be willing to admit that there are as many grades of literature as there are varieties and grades of the æsthetic sense in humanity. Bold as the position may appear to be, we are willing both to posit this and to admit this. All writings that have satisfied the critical requirements of past ages and the value of which is substantiated by the conservative academic critics of the present day, may be fairly said to satisfy the æsthetic sense of a typical reader — that is, of a man whose tastes are catholic and properly trained by education and by private study and reflection. Every critic, except the extreme impressionist perhaps, practically assumes that he is such a typical reader when he judges a book; and when the majority of critics, after due time has been allowed for the elimination of purely personal and temporary elements of criticism, agree on the literary character of the work in question, it may reasonably be said to satisfy the æsthetic sense of a typical reader.

On the other hand nothing can be plainer than that there are various grades of literature appealing to all classes of people and that the rigid critic and literary historian need not be frightened at the fact. For their purposes they have only to ascertain the verdict of the typical reader just described, and discuss or register that. This is practically what they do now, and they need not give themselves any more concern about the novels of Mr. E. P. Roe and Miss Marie Corelli than they do about the yellow-backed fiction sold on our railway trains or the continued stories that figure in the sensational journals. If, however, they are interested in the more or less philosophical aspects of literary study, they will find it hard to refute the claim that the novels of Mr. Roe and

Miss Corelli are popular with certain readers for practically the same reasons for which the novels of Scott, Balzac, Tolstoi, and Mr. Howells are popular with readers of higher æsthetic development — viz., that they make primarily a pleasurable appeal to the æsthetic emotions. We may call the novels of the latter writers literature, and of the former writers stuff, if we choose; but logically we have no more right to say that the two classes of fiction differ generically than we have to say that the inhabitants of Murray Hill are human beings and those of the Bowery mere brutes. We find it necessary to divide mankind into social classes, and thus for purposes of criticism and education we divide literature into various grades and consider only the higher ones; but this should not blind us to the unity that in both cases underlies our division.[1]

We conclude, therefore, that our tests are elastic rather than too easy, and we shall bring our discussion to a close by remarking that by making free use of our elastic tests we shall not only be better able to sympathize with the literary tastes of people of inferior

[1] See on this point Mr. Brander Matthews' valuable essay On Pleasing the Taste of the Public, in his Aspects of Fiction.

culture, and so be able to help them to rise in the scale of taste and intelligence, but also be more certain to comprehend and supply the literary needs of children, whether they are our own or else are confided to our guidance. The teaching as well as the criticism of pure literature will be greatly improved from the moment teachers and critics pay more attention to the emotive than to the intellectual qualities of literature, from the moment they begin to ask what literature does rather than what it is.

V

ON TRANSLATING HORACE

V

ON TRANSLATING HORACE

THAT to attempt to translate Horace is to attempt the impossible is a statement that has long since passed into a proverb, of which no one makes greater use than the Horatian translator himself. Perhaps we owe to this proverbial impossibility the fact that the translator of Horace is always with us. A living, breathing antinomy, he writes a modest preface, then, muttering to himself " *nil mortalibus ardui est*," he tries to scale very heaven in his folly, to rush blindly "*per vetitum nefas*." But because he has loved much, therefore shall much be forgiven him. If Horace were not Horace, his translators would be more successful, but surely they would be fewer in number. To love Horace passionately and not try to translate him would be to flout that principle of altruism in which Mr. Kidd discovers, poetically though not philosophically, the motive force of civilization. "We love Horace, therefore we must endeavor to set him forth in a way to make others love him," is what all translators say to themselves, consciously or unconsciously, when they decide to publish their respective renditions. And who shall blame them? For where is the critic, competent to judge their work, who has not himself listened to the Siren's song, if but for a moment in his youth, who has not a version of some Horatian ode hid away in his portfolio, the memory of which will forever prevent him from flinging stones at his fellow offenders?

But, if to translate Horace be impossible, it is hardly less impossible to explain fully the causes of his unbounded popularity. Admirers of Lucretius and Catullus tell us very plainly that he is not a great poet, but somehow we do not resent the charge; we only read him, if possible, more diligently and affectionately. We leave our critical faculties in abeyance when Dante [1] introduces him to us along with Homer and Ovid and Lucan, and our hearts tell us that he is, in the truest sense, worthy to walk with the greatest of these companions. We feel sure that Virgil must have loved him as a man; we have proof that Milton loved him as a poet. We deny to him "the grand manner," but we attribute to him every charm. When we seek to analyze this charm, we find that where

[1] *Inferno*, I., 89.

we can point out ten of its elements, such as wit, humor, vivacity, sententiousness, kindliness, and the like, there are ten others, equally potent but more subtle, that escape us altogether. So we turn the saying of Buffon into "the charm is the man," and contentedly exchange analysis for enjoyment. And yet we are firmly persuaded that no author is more worthy of the painstaking study characteristic of modern scholarship than is this same Epicurean poet, who so utterly defies analysis and would be the first to smile at our ponderous erudition. We feel that the scholar who should devote the best years of his life to studying the influence of Horace upon subsequent literatures, and to collecting the tributes that have been paid to his genius by the great and worthy of all lands and ages, would deserve our heartfelt benedictions.[1] We conclude, in short, that that most exquisite of epithets, "the well-beloved," so inappropriately bestowed upon the worthless and flippant French king, belongs to Horace and to Horace alone, *jure divino*.

We are concerned here, however, rather with Horace's translators than with Horace

---

[1] See in this connection the eloquent paragraph in Sir Theodore Martin's Works of Horace, vol. i., p. 182.

himself, for my purpose is to say a few words about the methods of rendering the poet that have most commended themselves of recent years. So much has been written upon this subject and so much remains to be written, that it is hard to determine where to begin; but I fancy that the preface of the late Professor Conington to his well-known translation of the Odes will furnish a proper point of departure. Few persons, whether translators or readers, can object to Conington's first premise that the translator ought to aim at "some kind of metrical conformity to his original." To reproduce an original Sapphic or Alcaic in blank verse, or in the couplet of Pope, is to repel at once the reader who knows his Horace, and to give the reader who is ignorant of Latin a totally erroneous conception of the rhythmical method of the poet. To render a compressed Latin verse by a diffuse English one is, as Conington points out, to do injustice to the sententiousness for which Horace is justly celebrated,—although it must be remarked that the translator should not, in order to avoid diffuseness, be led astray as Mr. Gladstone was recently by the "fatal facility" of the octosyllabic couplet. To translate Horace, except on occasions, into anything but quatrains, is also to handicap one's reader heavily from the metrical point of view. It seems to me, however, that when Professor Conington insisted that an English measure once adopted for the Alcaic must be used for every ode in which Horace employed the latter stanza — a practice which Mr. Gladstone avoided — he went far toward handicapping the translator, who, after all, has his rights. That such uniformity ought to be aimed at, and will be aimed at, is doubtless true; but there is one element of the problem with which Professor Conington did not sufficiently reckon. This is rhyme, which he assumes to be necessary at present to a successful rendition of a Horatian ode. A uniform rhymeless stanza can probably be applied to all odes in a particular measure without any special loss resulting. But this can hardly be the case with a rhyming stanza, if the translator aim, as he should do, at a fairly, though not meticulously, literal rendering of his original and not at the paraphrasing which so often satisfied Mr. Gladstone. There will necessarily be coincidences of sound in a literal prose version of a Latin stanza that will suggest a particular arrangement of rhymes for a poetical version. To adopt a uniform English stanza is to do away with this natural advantage, which presents itself to the translator oftener than might be supposed.

A concrete example will suffice to make my meaning clear. The third ode of the First Book, the well-known *Sic te diva potens Cypri*, is in what is called the Second Asclepiad metre; so is the delightful third ode of the Ninth Book, the *Donec gratus eram tibi*. We will assume that the translator has chosen for the *Sic te diva*, a quatrain with alternating rhymes. Following Professor Conington's rule of uniformity, he must employ the same stanza for the *Donec gratus eram*, which, by the way, Conington did not do for reasons he explained at length. Now the sixth stanza of the latter ode runs as follows:

> " Quid si prisca redit Venus
>   Diductosque jugo cogit aëneo,
>   Si flava excutitur Chloë,
>   Rejectaeque patet janua Lydiae."

This may be translated:

" What if the former love return and join with brazen yoke the parted ones, if yellow-haired Chloë be shaken off, and the door stand open for rejected Lydia?"

If my memory does not deceive me, it was this stanza, and especially one word in its last verse, that determined the arrangement of rhymes in a version I attempted years ago, Consule Planco. This verse seemed to run inevitably into

"And open stand for Lydia the *door*."

It needed but a moment to detect in the first verse of the stanza a sufficient rhyme. The syllable *re* of *reducit* furnished *more*, not perhaps the most apt of rhymes with *door*, but still sufficient, as things go with translators, and with a pardonable tautology I wrote —

"What if the former love once more
    Return —"

Two other rhymes were found with little difficulty in the *di* of *diductos* and in *excutitur*, which suggested *wide* and *cast aside*, and the whole stanza appeared, omitting strictly metrical considerations, as follows:

"What if the former love once more
    Return and yoke the lovers parted wide,
    If Chloë, yellow-haired, be cast aside,
And open stand for Lydia the door?"

This stanza certainly had the merit of literalness — it omitted only the rather unessential epithet *rejectae* and compressed the phrase *jugo cogit aëneo* — and I thought it had some merits of rhythm and diction. So I took it as a model, and, with little difficulty, translated the remainder of the ode — with what amount of total success there is no need of discussing here.

This example, with many more, has confirmed me in my belief not only that uniformity of measure is not to be insisted upon strictly in the case of rhyming stanzas, but also that translators should search more thoroughly than they seem to do, for what I may call the rhyme suggestions that are implicit in so many Horatian stanzas. I am convinced that any translator who, having adopted a quatrain with alternating rhymes for the *Sic te diva*, should persist in rejecting a quatrain with internal rhymes for the *Donec gratus eram*, simply because he was bent on preserving uniformity, would be hampering himself and doing an injustice to his original.

Upon other points it is easier to agree with Professor Conington. For a majority of the odes, the iambic movement, which is natural to English, is preferable. This Milton seems to have seen, his disuse of rhyme in his celebrated version of the *Quis multa gracilis* (i., 5) having given him an opportunity for experiment in logaœdic verse, of which he did not avail himself. Here, too, however, I must plead for a careful study of each ode by the translator, for I think that there are cases in which it would be almost disastrous to attempt an iambic rendering. Such a case is presented, perhaps, by the " *Diffugere nives* " (iv., 7). The iambic renderings of Professor Conington and Sir Theodore Martin seem to me to stray far from the original movement — as far as the former's:

"'No 'scaping death' proclaims the year"

does from the diction of Horace or of any other poet. Both would have done better to transfer as far as they could the Latin movement to their English renderings. It is true that English dactyls are dangerous things, especially in translations, where the padding or " packing " which is natural to them, is increased by the padding natural to a translation from a synthetic into an analytic language; but the dactylic movement of the First Archilochian, in which the *Diffugere nives* is written, is hardly to be transferred into English iambics at all. It presents more difficulty than the transference of the movement of hexameters proper into our blank verse.

Where the translator, however, makes up his mind to attempt a close approximation to the classical metre, I am of the opinion that he should eschew the use of rhyme as too foreign to his original. But, since the use of rhyme seems, as Conington holds, to be essential at present, if the English version is to be acceptable as poetry, this close approximation can be desirable in a few special cases only. It will not do to dogmatize on such matters, but it may be safely said that no poet has yet accustomed the English ear to the use of rhymeless verse in lyrical poetry. What some future master may accomplish is another matter. Here and there a successful rhymeless lyric like Collins's famous Ode to Evening, or Tennyson's Alcaics on Milton, shows us that rhymeless stanzas may be used in lyric poetry with great effect; but so far the translators of Horace that have eschewed rhyme have failed as a rule, like the late Lord Lytton, to give us versions that charm. Yet charm is what they should chiefly endeavor to convey.

I am still more convinced that Professor Conington is right when he insists that the English should be confined " within the same number of lines as the Latin." He is surely right when he taxes Sir Theodore Martin, who so frequently violates this rule, with an exuberance that is totally at variance with the severity of the classics. This exuberance is almost certain to make its presence felt if the translator abandon the strict number of the lines into which Horace has compressed his thought. It results, too, from a division into stanzas of over four veses. There is no rule of translation that will so effectively insure a successful retention of the diction of the original as this of the line for line rendering. And that the diction and the thought of the poet should be more closely followed than is usually the case, admits of no manner of doubt. I have already said that a close scrutiny of the original will often suggest an almost literal rendering of the thought and diction. This literal rendering is naturally more desired by the reader who is familiar with Horace than by the reader who is not, but it will be both pleasing and serviceable to the latter, if not too slavishly obtained. Metrical considerations and general smoothness ought to weigh with every translator, but they ought not to outweigh accurate rendering of diction and thought. In this connection I am not at all sure that Conington does not go too far when he recommends the Horatian translator to hold by the diction of our own Augustan period. That the age of Pope corresponds in many respects with that of Horace is, of course, true enough, and the student of eighteenth century English poetry is almost sure to be an admirer of the Roman " bard " so fashionable at the time. But Horace's diction does not strike us as stilted, while Pope's often does; and for a modern translator to indulge in stilted diction is fatal not only to the intrinsic value of his work, but also to its popularity and hence to its present effectiveness. There is a good deal, too, about our poetry of the eighteenth century that is little short of commonplace; but commonplace the translator of Horace can least afford to be. Horace may approach dangerously near the commonplace, yet he always misses it by a dexterous and graceful turn. The translator, running after, will miss this turn often enough as it is; he cannot, therefore afford to steep himself in a literature that has a tendency to the commonplace.

To mention the eighteenth century and Horace is to bring up the thought of Horatian paraphrases. A successful paraphrase is oftentimes better as poetry than a good poetical translation, and not infrequently gives a fuller idea of Horace's spirit. It is almost needless to praise the work in this kind of Mr. Austin Dobson and Mr. Eugene Field. But a paraphrase, however good, can never be entirely satisfying either to the reader that knows Horace or to the reader that desires to know him.   Nor can a prose version be thoroughly satisfactory.   What is wanted is not merely the drift of the poet's thought, but so far as is possible what he actually sang.   The paraphrase may sing, and the prose version may give us the thought in nearly equivalent words, but neither answers our desires so well as a good poetical translation does — such a translation, let us say, as Professor Goldwin Smith's of the *Cælo tonantem* (iii., 5). Yet there is surely room for these three methods of rendering, and just as surely one could write indefinitely on the whole fascinating subject did not one consult the interests of Horace and of one's readers.

VI

THE BYRON REVIVAL

THE BYRON REVIVAL

IT is now some years since the late Prof. Nichol, in his excellent life of Byron, declared that his hero was " resuming his place," and that the closing quarter of the century would reverse the unjust verdict against him pronounced by the second and third quarters. Shortly after this statement was made, Matthew Arnold, as though to confirm its truth, published his well-known volume of selections from Byron's poetry, and maintained in his preface that when the year 1900 should be turned, the two chief names of modern English poetry would be those of Wordsworth and Byron. To the latter claim, Mr. Swinburne immediately replied, in what purported to be a critical essay on the two poets just named, but was really a marvellous dithyramb of inveterate prejudice.

As might have been expected, Mr. Swinburne, too, had a pair of chief poets to set up — to wit, Shelley and Coleridge. The controversy thus begun received some attention from the critics; but the general public was more interested in reading Tennyson and in forming Browning clubs. If the tide of favor began setting toward Byron, its movement was practically imperceptible; for as late as 1896 Prof. George Saintsbury could maintain, without serious loss to his reputation as a critic, that Scott could not be ranked below Byron on any sound theory of poetical criticism, and that the latter could not be read in close juxtaposition with a real poet like Shelley without disastrous results to his fame.

Twelve months later, however, Byron was being more discussed, if not more read. The war between Greece and Turkey naturally induced men to ponder upon his disinterested devotion to the cause of Hellas and upon the glorious close of his wayward life. The newspapers took him up; and certainly those of Paris, where I happened to be at the time, did not bear out the opinion afterward expressed to me by an eminent French critic, who was doubtless in the right, that the influence of Byron had somewhat waned in France.

Close upon this transient notoriety came an important proof that the great poet's fame was not destitute of champions in his native land after the death of Matthew Arnold. The first volume of a critical edition of his complete works, under the editorship of Mr. W. E. Henley, was issued and cordially received; and it was announced that Mr. John Murray would shortly draw on his stores of manuscripts, and publish an edition that should be practically final. Accordingly we now have Mr. Henley's edition of the Letters from 1804 to 1813, and two volumes of the Murray edition — one containing the earlier poems, edited by Mr. Ernest Hartley Coleridge, and one containing Letters dating from 1798 to 1811, edited by Mr. Rowland E. Prothero. Both editions are to be in twelve volumes; and the publishers promise to complete them without loss of time.

The simultaneous appearance of two such rival editions would be noteworthy in the case of any poet, but is particularly remarkable in the case of Byron. As Mr. Henley says, his own is " practically the first reissue on novel and peculiar lines which has been attempted for close on seventy years." There have been innumerable popular editions of Byron to satisfy a demand which some booksellers pronounce constant, but others declare to be falling off; yet, to the present year, if any one wished to do critical work on the poet, he had to resort mainly to the seventeen-volume Murray edition of 1832. The general excellence of this may partly account for the fact that in an age famous for textual criticism Byron did not receive until recently an honor long ago paid to Shelley and Wordsworth and Keats; but one can hardly help believing that popular and critical indifference was chiefly responsible for the neglect. Now, however, that in this important particular he is receiving his own with interest, it may be well to take a nearer view of the rival editions.

That of Mr. Murray is clearly the only one entitled to call itself complete: it is equally clear that he has been unfortunate in not securing Mr. Henley to edit it, with Mr. Prothero to edit Mr. Henley. Mr. Prothero has done his work well; he prints eighty more letters for the same space of time than Mr. Henley; but, as he gracefully acknowledges, he cannot handle his materials in the attractive way his rival can. Mr. Henley's notes abound in errors, but are almost as interesting as the letters he annotates, — which is saying a great deal; for Byron, with his dash, directness, and force, ranks near the very top of the world's great letter-writers.

Mr. Henley's editorial success has a two-fold source — first, his devotion to Byron, whom he considers to be " the sole English poet (for Sir Walter conquered in prose) bred since Milton to live a master influence in the world at large," and second, his intimate knowledge of the England of the Regency, whose hidebound, but corrupt, society could tolerate Castlereagh and Yarmouth and the Prince himself, but drove Byron into exile. His knowledge and love of his subject are indeed so great that one would almost acknowledge him as an ideal editor, in spite of his talent for unscholarly, if trifling, blunders, did not one discover in his work a certain lack of refinement that is disturbing. For example, there was really no necessity for him to denominate Pierce Egan an " ass," or the quack that tortured Byron's foot an " ignorant brute." But, notwithstanding such blemishes and the normal assertiveness of his manner, there can be little doubt that Mr. Henley's will long remain a most interesting edition of Byron for the general reader.

This is not to say, however, that the handsome Murray edition is valuable only because it is complete and, apparently, final. Mr. Prothero has annotated the letters most carefully; and I cannot agree with those critics who think that he should have cast aside some of his materials. There are comparatively few of the social notes and letters included that do not throw light on Byron's character; and nearly all are interesting. The latter statement cannot be made, of course, for the early poems, which Mr. Coleridge has annotated with scholarly thoroughness. It will take the verve of Mr. Henley's notes to make the Hours of Idleness go down. I have re-read these youthful verses: and the only pleasure I could get from them lay in the fact that the various readings collated by the new editor seemed to show that, on the whole, when Byron altered a verse, he improved it — whence I derived a vague, but perhaps vain, hope that succeeding volumes will enable us to think a little better of him as a technical artist than most of us, whether we admire him or not, are now able to do.

The eleven fresh poems printed by Mr. Coleridge do not help matters out in the least; but this need not take the relish from the news that fifteen stanzas of Don Juan

and a fairly large fragment of the third part
of The Deformed Transformed are to be
given us in due season. It is a pity, from
the point of view of those who intend to use
this edition to re-read their Byron slowly,
that the publishers did not wait until two
volumes of the poetry were ready. Even
the English Bards and Scotch Reviewers,
though it be admitted to be the best strictly
literary satire between The Dunciad and
A Fable for Critics, cannot neutralize the
deadly effect of the Hours of Idleness
and give life to this first of the six volumes
that are to contain Byron's poetry. I know
of no other poet of eminence who is so
handicapped by his youthful verses. Others
have written stuff as worthless, or even worse;
but no other that I can recall has barred
the way to his great achievements by such
a mass of uniformly immature and mediocre
work. This has been said and thought
thousands of times, to be sure, since the
Edinburgh printed its needlessly harsh
critique and stung Byron's genius into life;
but it does not seem to have suggested,
either to editors or to publishers, the propriety, in popular editions at least, of beginning the poetical works with the English
Bards and printing the early verses as an

appendix. We are constantly laboring to facilitate approach to our poets, we compile volumes of selections, we introduce them and annotate them; yet we seldom adopt this easy and useful plan of putting their *impedimenta* in the rear.

But have these two editions stimulated a real Byron revival, or can any rearrangement of his works make him genuinely popular once more among English readers? I cannot, with the best wish to persuade myself, believe that any permanent reaction in his favor has as yet set in, nor am I at all confident that he will ever be read with the old enthusiasm by all classes of people. My reasons for these opinions cannot be given without some discussion of his much-mooted rank as a poet; but, as the point in question is one of real critical importance, and as the present is a particularly opportune time, I shall not shrink from taking part in what may seem at first thought to be a hopelessly involved controversy.

Byron, as we all know, was acknowledged by his contemporaries, both at home and abroad, to be the master poet of his generation. He has practically lost this position in the eyes of English-speaking peoples, but has kept it among Continental peoples. Taine and Castelar and Elze place him at the summit of poetic renown, much as Goethe did over seventy years ago. No Englishman, however, not even Matthew Arnold, writes of him so enthusiastically as Sir Walter Scott could do in all sincerity. The reaction against him set in shortly after his death, Carlyle giving it potent voice; and to-day Wordsworth, Shelley, Keats, Tennyson, and Browning can count their partisans by scores, where Byron can count one.

Nor is it merely a question of his relative rank among nineteenth-century poets. Such critics as Mr. Swinburne, Mr. Saintsbury, and Mr. Lionel Johnson have practically denied him any standing at all as a great poet; and even his stanch admirers feel called upon to qualify their praise. When Arnold extolled him at the expense of Shelley, the critics, great and little, took a professional pleasure in charging their leader with being for once thoroughly erratic.

Many reasons have been brought forward to account for this change of taste and opinion among Englishmen. Byron's enemies say that we are more clear-sighted than our grandfathers were, that we have stripped the masks from his Laras and Conrads and Manfreds, and exposed the tawdry pseudo-poet beneath; that we know better than to receive a traveller's versified note-book as an inspired poem; that, if he has any merit at all, it is merely as a satirist and a rhetorician. Less rabid critics call attention to the fact, that, after the strenuous Revolutionary period was over, Englishmen felt the need of calmer, more moral, and more artistic poetry, and that what was Tennyson's opportunity was naturally Byron's extremity. In a critical, neo-Alexandrian age, they say, the poet who wrote just as passion and impulse dictated can find no appreciative audience save among the semi-cultured. On the Continent the case is different, because foreigners are naturally blind to artistic defects that are patent to every Englishman, and Byron's force and passion can produce their legitimate effects unhindered, much as they did among our forefathers, who were living in a transitional poetic period, and were, moreover, dazzled by the fiery personality of the man.

There can be little doubt that the moderate views just given contain much that is true. I will go further and say that they are practically the grounds on which I rest my belief that no genuine revival of Byron will be possible among us for a long time to come. We are, as a rule, too sophisticated, too

Alexandrian in our tastes, to enjoy greatly poetry that is thrown off at a white heat, save perhaps, for variety, the ballads with which Mr. Kipling has been favoring us. We prefer the artistic, the carefully wrought; and, even so, we do not desire that the poet's art should be as strenuous as it is in Paradise Lost. Until something stirs us up as a race, Byron is likely to be a favorite only with youths who are naturally passionate and with disillusioned men who can get pleasure out of wit and satire.

But reasons that apply to the mass of readers do not necessarily apply to critics and men of more than ordinary culture. Such persons ought to be able to rid themselves, to some extent, of the prejudices of their own age and to fit themselves to enjoy genuine poetic merit of every sort. If it be true that Byron possessed a splendid personality, the force, the passion, the sincerity of which have been transmitted to his work, it is a sign of weakness when the cultured man of to-day fails to enjoy these qualities, because, forsooth, he is offended by a false note here, a glaring patch of color there. There seems, too, to be an inherent weakness in our critical methods, if we can neglect, misunderstand, or treat with contempt a writer who was believed by his contemporaries to have dominated their age, and from whom foreigners have gathered literary inspiration for nearly a century. In other words, while there may be good reason to believe that a popular reaction in Byron's favor is not to be looked for shortly, is there any reason to believe that a majority of our critics and men of culture must continue to keep their faces turned away from him, as seems to be the case at present?

I am inclined to answer, No. Byron's case with the critics is by no means so hopeless as the comparative failure of Matthew Arnold's defence of him would seem to prove. This is, on the whole, an age in which criticism is in the hands of impressionists and scholars; that is to say, most men who write about literary matters are critics of taste or critics of knowledge. Above these two classes, unifying and correlating their respective qualities, are to be found the critics of judgment, who are naturally not numerous at any period. Matthew Arnold belonged to this last class; and some of his judgments, particularly those relating to Byron and Shelley, were unintelligible to Mr. Swinburne and Mr. Saintsbury, among others, simply because, as critics of taste and of knowledge, respectively, they were better fitted to play the advocate than to judge. Now judgment has always characterized the Continental critics, especially the French, more than it has the English; and when we find men like Taine, Elze, and Castelar practically agreeing in their estimates of Byron, it ought to make us pause. A cultivated taste means much; wide and accurate knowledge means much: but the impressionists and scholars have between them managed to get English criticism into an almost anarchical state; and the time is probably not far distant when the higher claims of the critics of judgment will be acknowledged with relief, even at the risk of the establishment of a dictatorial power like that of Dr. Johnson. Such a dogmatic reign as his will not, of course, be seen again; but chaos at least will not be long tolerated. And when anarchy ends among the critics, Byron may come once more into favor, for the following reasons, which I submit not as my own, — that would be presumptuous in view of what I have just written, — but as gathered by me from my reading of the critics, and tested by a recent reperusal of the whole of Byron's poetical work.

Mr. Henley calls Byron the " voice-in-chief" of his generation; and such was the opinion of contemporaries like Sir Walter Scott and Shelley. Hatred of established conventions, political, religious, and social; love for nature in her wilder aspects; romantic fervor in personal attachments; lack of reticence in the expression of emotions, — in short, a fervid individualism, may be said to have been the leavening characteristics of the age; and they plainly received their fullest utterance in Byron's poetry. He may, therefore, be called legitimately the poet of an age; but we should not pay him the honors due to this high class of poets until we have measured him with Dante or Shakspere or Milton, and determined whether he is also a poet for all time. His present obscuration does not absolve us from this comparison; for there have been times when even Dante's fame has been somewhat obscured in Italy.

The immediate effects of such a comparison cannot but be disastrous to Byron. He has not the high moral earnestness of Dante or Milton; he has not their intellectual scope; he has not their invariably perfect style. Whether as man or poet, he is at once seen to be far their inferior; and, if we were to confine our attention to his conduct or to his marvellously erratic judgments about men and books, it would seem to be an impertinence to mention his name along with those of such consummate masters. Yet he voiced the best of his age, and possessed a personality of transcendent force. Are we, therefore, quite sure that the comparison we are instituting is unnecessary? Have we not omitted to consider some essential element?

We have. The great poets, "not of an age, but for all time," have all left masterpieces in which their genius has taken a long and sustained flight, — masterpieces each in its way unapproachable. Has Byron left any such? He has, in Don Juan, and its pendants, Beppo and The Vision of Judgment. These great poems are, to be sure, vastly inferior to The Divine Comedy, Othello, and Paradise Lost; but Don Juan, at least, is akin to them in being a work of sustained poetic imagination, perfect of its sort, unapproachable, and perennially fresh. It voices its author and his age; it is *sui generis*, the greatest of humorous epics, couched in a style that could not be changed except for the worse, and unique in its combination of wit, humor, and satire with a genuine and rich vein of romantic and descriptive poetry. It is, in my opinion, the single sustained work of poetic imagination produced in nineteenth-century England that keeps a level flight, the only one written in a style and verse-form as absolutely appropriated by its author as English blank verse is by Milton, the Latin hexameter by Virgil, and the Romantic Alexandrine by Victor Hugo. I will go further and say that, to me at least, it is the single long poem in English since Paradise Lost that grows fresher with each reading and that gives me the sense of being in the presence of a spirit of almost boundless capacity. If this spirit does not soar into the heaven of heavens, it at least never falls to earth (save from the point of view of morals), but preserves a strong and middle flight.

What has just been claimed for Don Juan is practically what many critics have seen and said; but they have not, as a rule, made sufficient use of Byron's masterpiece to connect him with the great world-poets on the one hand, or to separate him, on the other, from his English contemporaries and successors. Elze, indeed, has placed him in a supreme position as representing " lyrical verse conceived in its widest sense as subjective poetry" (" die Lyrik im weitesten Sinne als subjective Poesie aufgefasst "); but this is a rather dangerous stand to take, both because the great world-poets have not won their position by their lyrical work, and because Byron's lyrical efforts, whether in a technical or a broader sense, are often so faulty that to proclaim him as a supreme lyrist is practically to assert that he was a great poet because he was a great personality. It is safer to argue that the poets of the highest class are always represented by sustained masterpieces, and that Don Juan is sufficiently such a work to warrant our placing its author, who also voiced the aspirations of his age and was a tremendous personality, among the world-poets, but beneath them all in rank.

Applying now this "masterpiece" test to the much-disputed question of Byron's relative position among the English poets of this century, we must perhaps conclude that even Matthew Arnold has not made sufficient use of it. He has had a discerning eye for the beauty and value of the poetical passages scattered profusely through Byron's works, just as he has had for the similar passages in Wordsworth; but he has seemingly failed to consider architectonics, and has thus given the palm to Wordsworth on the just score of the superior quality of the latter's work when at its best. But where is Wordsworth's indisputable sustained masterpiece? Even the

Ode on the Intimations of Immortality has serious competitors, and, with all its beauty and power, does not connect its author with the world-poets. The Excursion has not won its way in England yet, much less on the Continent; and he would be a rash Wordsworthian who should assert that it ever will. And what have Keats and Coleridge to show in the way of masterpieces, such as we are considering? What has Shelley, whose Prometheus Unbound and The Cenci, though in some respects wonderful, are neither fully unique nor representative? As for the Idylls of the King and The Ring and the Book, one can merely say that they are still under the fire of the critics, and that the former, at least, is not likely to be pronounced unique or masterful, except by persons who know little about other heroic poetry.

According to the above reasoning, if the serried hosts of the partisans of other poets will allow the word to pass, it would seem that Byron is connected with the world-poets in three respects: he has written a sustained masterpiece; he is a representative character who has been accepted by the world at large; and he possesses a tremendously powerful personality. No other modern Englishman

is so connected with the world-poets; but
Byron himself falls below them in respect to
the inferior nature of his masterpiece and of
his own moral, intellectual and artistic qualifications.   Yet there is also another, though
a secondary, feature of his work that binds
him to the masters, and distinguishes him
from most of his contemporaries and successors — I mean the wide scope taken by
his versatility.   A discussion of this point
will naturally lead us to take a rapid survey
of his entire poetical achievement.

Passing over the Hours of Idleness, it is
to be noted that as early as 1808 Byron was
capable of a fine lyric. When We Two
Parted dates from this year, and breathes a
spirit of passionate sorrow hardly equalled in
literature; yet the major part of the lyrics of
this and the next few years cannot be said to
be of a high order.   There are some good
occasional verses, and Maid of Athens, I
Enter thy Garden of Roses, There be None
of Beauty's Daughters, rank very high; the
last-named being fully worthy of Shelley at
his best: but, although the general level of
the Hours of Idleness is surpassed, no
solid foundation for fame has yet been laid,
even if the verve of the English Bards be
taken into account.   In 1812 the stanzas to

Thyrza, beginning, "And thou art dead, as young and fair," showed what Byron might do in the elegy if he had a mind; and in 1815 the Hebrew Melodies, with their one supreme lyric (She Walks in Beauty), and at least three admirable songs, gave any one the right to expect great things of him as a lyrist. A little later his domestic troubles occasioned the writing of Fare Thee Well, and the three poems addressed to Augusta; but, after the later cantos of Childe Harold, the dramas, the final tales, and Don Juan began to occupy his mind, lyrical work became a matter of minor importance. He did not eschew it, of course; for Manfred and other dramatic poems required it; and here and there he wrote an excellent, though hardly a perfect, song. Even in Don Juan he made room for the eloquent Isles of Greece; and at Missolonghi itself he composed those stanzas on his thirty-sixth birthday which will be forgotten only when men cease to remember the nobly pathetic death that soon after befell him.

Taken in its totality, his lyric work must rank far below that of Shelley and Burns, to name no others; but it requires little critical discernment to perceive that he was capable of pushing any of his rivals close, if he had cared to put forth his full powers. It is idle to affirm that the man who wrote some of the doggerel in Heaven and Earth could never have been a true lyrist. The aberrations of men of genius, even of almost consummate artists, are not to be accounted for; and there are things perilously near doggerel in the mature work of poets like Shelley and Tennyson. Byron's aberrations in the matter of bad lyrical work are probably more distressing than those of any other great poet; but they are to be accounted for rather by the restlessness of his temperament than by his native incapacity to write a true song. He was much besides a lyric poet; but in gauging his versatility we must not overlook his undeveloped, but genuine, gift for singing, nor the absolute worth of at least a score of his lyrics.

Byron's contemporary fame took firm root with the publication of the first two cantos of Childe Harold in 1812. It is difficult now to understand how he could " awake and find himself famous " for such far from supreme work; but we must remember that people had had time to grow somewhat weary of Sir Walter's metrical romances of Scotland, and that the day had not come for popular appreciation of Wordsworth.

And the first cantos of Harold, with all their affectations and imperfections, have many decided merits which are still visible in this day of reaction against them. The invocation to the second canto, and such passages as that beginning, " Fair Greece, sad relic of departed worth," will attract readers long after Mr. Swinburne's contemptuous depreciation of the entire poem shall have been forgotten. Besides there is in them a foreshadowing of the descriptive power that was to make the third and fourth cantos memorable. In short, although Byron needed to work off his crude energies in the Eastern tales, to be disgusted with the licentious and frivolous society of the Regency, and to be stirred to the depths by his domestic troubles, before his genius could be fully roused, there were abundant signs of the existence of that genius from the moment that Scott, with a prudent magnanimity, abdicated the throne of verse in his favor.

The Eastern tales that followed in quick succession, The Giaour, The Bride of Abydos, The Corsair, and Lara naturally increased his reputation, because they were eminently readable and because they seemed to be partly autobiographic. None knew what the wild young peer had done in the East; therefore, every one read the tales and speculated. The Byronic hero became quite a social personage, — a fact which has since led to not a little depreciation of this portion of the poet's works. We are now told that The Giaour is the only one of the early tales possessing a spark of life; and, while this is an exaggeration, it is impossible to deny that it was a good thing for Byron's fame when, by rapid working, he exhausted his Eastern vein. The Bride and The Corsair, however, contain several passages of imperishable beauty; and, much as the mystery and gloom of Lara may be out of fashion, it is hardly fair to deny the power and the literary influence of that romance in the couplets of Pope. And besides the poetical passages, there was a vigor of narration that somewhat made up for the marked poverty of characterization, and that preluded the more successful later tales and the supreme achievement of Don Juan. Indeed, Byron must have felt that he had a faculty for narration, since he wrote The Island as late as 1823.

The Siege of Corinth and Parisina appeared shortly after his marriage; while The Prisoner of Chillon and Mazeppa date respectively from 1816 and 1818. His mental and artistic growth was distinctly revealed in these pieces, the third of which has become classical. Although The Siege ends badly and contains much crude work, it is memorable for its descriptive strength; and there are some passages and scenes in both Parisina and Mazeppa that will perish only with the language. Even The Island, which has been declared to be a total failure by so well disposed a critic as Mr. J. A. Symonds, is such only in the first canto. It manages to throw a kind of Chateaubriand glamour over the South Sea Islands, and proves that, even after its author's hand had become subdued to the far from sentimental materials of Don Juan, it had not entirely lost its early cunning in romantic narrative. We must, therefore, conclude, in despite of the critics, that Byron's tales count for something in his life-work, and are another proof of his wonderful versatility.

It is worth while to note, that, just as the unfairness of his early critics stimulated Byron to achieve the first stage of his fame, so the clamors of society against him after his rupture with his wife incited him to the still higher achievement represented by the third and fourth cantos of Childe Harold. The poet has now practically become another

man, and has transported his readers to a
new world. His intellectual grasp has become firmer and larger; his artistic powers
have been strengthened and chastened, though
not to the height of perfection; and his emotions and passions have been keyed to a point
of intensity almost unparalleled. The result is
a series of marvellous passages, which need only
structural unity to make them a great poem.
The Spirit of Nature has seized hold upon
him, not through the influence of Wordsworth, as some suppose, but because of native
propensity and enforced disgust with the
world of men; and he rises to the supreme
heights of descriptive poetry. Some of his
stanzas devoted to the Alps are fairly sublime
with passion. He does not penetrate Nature, as
Wordsworth does: he appropriates her. And
he almost manages to move without tripping
over the fields of history and criticism, usually so foreign to him. He can characterize
Rousseau and Gibbon, can comprehend the
past of Italy and Rome, and can fairly con-
quer his normal ineptitude in matters of art.
As for the noble and exquisite land in which
he was to spend his exile, he almost appropriates her as he does Nature. The Italy of
Childe Harold, whatever artistic blemishes
that poem may have, has dominated the

world, certainly the English portion of it, in a manner not equalled by the subtler work of Landor or Shelley or Browning. It is this Italy that reappears in Parisina, in Beppo, in The Lament of Tasso, in The Prophecy of Dante, in the Ode on Venice, in certain of the dramas — and lends charm to them all. The Lament of Tasso has, indeed, a power all its own that forestalls Browning and that makes one question why it is not more highly esteemed; but The Two Foscari would be almost unreadable save for the passages that describe its hero's passion for Venice, loveliest of cities.

We can now see that the later narrative and descriptive work not only furnishes fresh proof of Bryon's astonishing versatility, but would suffice, without Don Juan, to give its author a very high, though not the supreme position among the English poets of this century. But the entire dramatic section of his writings, including no less than eight lyrical dramas and tragedies, remains to be considered.

It is usual to dismiss most of this work with positive contempt; but I, at least, must agree with Dr. Garnett in believing that Byron has, " like Dryden, produced memorable works by force and flexibility of genius." I will go further and say, that, after having just re-read them all, I should prefer to begin immediately to read them over again to being forced to go through once more the entire dramatic work of Tennyson or Browning. I am well aware that Byron's blank verse is often execrable, whether through his carelessness or his incapacity to handle that measure; I know that only that precious product of open plunder, Werner, succeeded on the stage; I admit that Byron's genius was essentially non-dramatic, that his chief characters are not real persons, but ideal personages; — I admit almost anything, in short, except the claim that the dramas are total, or nearly total, failures. Almost all carry interest; all show force and versatility; not one is lacking in passages of passion; and at least three are, with all their faults, productions not to be matched in the works of any of Byron's modern rivals, save Shelley. These three are Manfred, Cain, and Sardanapalus, which may be set beside the Prometheus Unbound and The Cenci. The British critics have almost unanimously rendered their verdict in favor of Shelley; and, from the point of view of technical art, they are doubtless in the right. Yet I question whether the sheer vigor of Byron does not balance the art of Shelley in a class of compositions in which neither could attain perfection.

But, when the dramas have been added to the lyrical, narrative, and descriptive work, to vindicate Byron's claim to be considered the most versatile poetic genius of modern England, we are brought full upon the masterpiece which of itself alone might suffice to prove the truth of this claim, that wonderful Don Juan, almost the only modern poem of which, adapting Shakspere, one may affirm that "age cannot wither it nor custom stale its infinite variety." I shall say little more about it, save to remark that its poetical passages have a *richer* tone than can easily be found elsewhere in Byron's own work or in that of his rivals, and that its fierce denunciation and irresistible ridicule of cant and tyranny ought to make it and its pendant, The Vision of Judgment, almost, if not quite, the master poems of modern democracy. Byron was a revolted aristocrat, it is true; but his acquired sympathy with democratic ideals, especially those of America, became a liberalizing force that can hardly be overpraised and should never be forgotten. We, at least, the countrymen of the Washington he extolled, should not be ungrateful to his memory; and the advocates of peace among the nations should hail him as their most effective champion.

But the reader may ask, What has become of the vicious, the irreligious Byron of our forefathers — the author of the blasphemous Cain and the licentious Don Juan, which no self-respecting man ought to read? An obvious answer to this question would be the statement that he never existed, save in the heated imaginations of his well-meaning, but unintelligent, countrymen. Such an answer, however, would smack partly of disingenuousness. It is true that the " monster of wickedness" never existed; but it is also true that Byron, by his conduct and his writings, sketched the outlines of a caricature which his countrymen had only to fill in. The high praise I have just given him as an apostle of liberty and peace is thoroughly deserved; and he died a martyr for freedom; but his life was in many important respects unworthy and low; his character was soiled by traits of vulgarity and vice; and his writings were often impure. Time has naturally softened us toward him; and study of him and his age has convinced us that there was far more of good than of bad in him, that much extenuation can be found for his conduct and the impurity of his writings: but, while we judge the man as leniently as we can, it would not be just to ourselves if we were to make as much allowance for his literary work, the influence of which lives on. We may, indeed, easily dismiss the charge of blasphemy; for the word has various meanings at various periods and to various orders of intelligence. Byron did not mean to be blasphemous; and his attitude toward Christianity is at most wavering, not positively sceptical or defiant. To eschew his poetry on this account, in an age that tolerates Mrs. Humphry Ward, would be little short of ridiculous in any person of even semi-culture.

The charge of impurity cannot be dismissed so easily, although it would hardly be raised against a foreign writer. Some of his earliest verse was suppressed, on account of its sensual tone, by his kind friend, Mr. Beecher. In the lyrical and narrative work written before his marriage he kept this vein under, but did not manage, and probably did not wish, to hide its existence. In the better portions of Childe Harold, in the dramas, even in such later tales as Parisina, it would require a prying purist to find anything seriously objectionable. In Beppo and Don Juan, however, he gave himself a loose rein, in spite of the importunities of La Guiccioli. He took delight in shocking the sense of propriety of his countrymen, who had treated him with injustice; but, while his heartiest admirers cannot but wish that he had not gone so far, they find in this very fact not only an excuse for him, but a safe means of rescuing the two poems from the mass of pornographic and lubricous literature. Certain scenes and passages of Don Juan are not deliberate efforts to corrupt: they are rather the ebullitions of a coarse, but thoroughly sincere, satirist, bent on shocking people he despises. The wit, the verve, the humor, the satire that are explicit or implicit in almost every stanza save Don Juan so as by fire.

The London of the Regency naturally could not take this view of the matter, and sought to drown its own shame in the clamor that it raised over the alleged immorality of the new poem; but choice and wholesome spirits, like Sir Walter Scott, saw that Byron had struck his true vein, and cheered him on. As the cantos proceeded, he held himself in more and more, so that much of the poem is practically unamenable to censure. And now that time has removed us as far from him as he was from Fielding, it would seem that only those who are peculiarly sensitive to the coarse, and peculiarly insensitive to wit, need be warned away from the greatest masterpiece of its kind in any literature.

In short, just as an age that tolerates Mrs. Ward need not fear that Byron will sap its faith, so an age that reads without abhorrence certain chapters in The Manxman, in Jude the Obscure, and in Evelyn Innes, cannot with consistency put Don Juan beyond the pale. Nor should an age that admires brilliant achievements of all kinds long withhold its praise from that wonderfully passionate, strong, and sincere soul which, after uttering itself in the master poem and poetry of a tremendous epoch, gave itself up a willing sacrifice to the cause of human freedom in the fatal marshes of Missolonghi.

VII

TEACHING THE SPIRIT OF LITERATURE

VII

TEACHING THE SPIRIT OF LITERATURE.

READERS of Balzac's Une Fille d'Ève will recall his description of the depressing education given by the Countess de Granville to her two young daughters. That she might make smooth their path to heaven and matrimony, she subjected them to a regimen that had at least one fatal defect, in that it took no account of their emotions. Its results may be learned from the story, but few thoughtful readers will refrain from asking themselves whether our educational regimen is not in too many cases followed by results similar in kind, if not in degree.

Parents and teachers of modern America have doubtless quite different ideals for their children from those of the Countess de Granville, but they often make the mistake that she did of pursuing these ideals at the cost of their children's emotions; that is to say, at the cost of their real happiness. The ideals of the French mother were summed up in the word *convenance* ; the ideals of too many American mothers and fathers, and, I regret to add, teachers, are summed up in the word " utility." Neither set of idcals takes much account of those emotions which are the highest part of our nature, and are most impressionable in childhood; for the world of the suitable and of the useful is the world of fact, and fact has to be transmuted by the imagination before it can reach and act upon the emotions. It follows, then, that every educational regimen which appeals to the mind through facts should be supplemented by one which appeals to the soul through ideas; that is, through facts transmuted by the imagination. Hence no educational system is complete that does not include instruction in religion and art, the two chief sources of appeal to the emotions. For obvious reasons we Americans have been compelled to leave religion outside the ordinary school and college curriculum, and this is practically the case with the plastic arts. We are thus reduced to rely mainly on literature and music as sources of appeal to the emotions of our youth, but we have hitherto made insufficient use of both.

This was not the case with the best educated people the world has ever known, the Greeks. Literature, especially poetry, and music were the basis of a Greek boy's education, and education in these two arts (which it must be remembered were closely connected with religion) led to the culmination of all the other arts in the Athens of Pericles. But the Athens of Pericles had its weakness as well as its strength, and the world has moved forward greatly in twenty-three hundred years; hence the basis of a boy's education should be far broader now than it was then. Yet while broadening the base and shifting its centre, we should not be rash enough to cast away its old material. Poetry and music are still essential to any sound educational system; and this being so, the inquiry how they may best be taught is of great interest, and, if confined to the first named, leads to the main topic of this paper.

I use the term "poetry" advisedly, for it best represents the literature of the imagination, and that is what we have to deal with, as we shall see at once after a little analysis. What did the Greek teacher expect his pupils to get from their study of Homer? Probably two sets of good results; one affecting the mind, the other the soul. From the

Iliad and the Odyssey the Greek boy could derive much information with regard to mythology, genealogy, and so-called history. They served also as reading-books, and for a long while took the place of formal grammars and treatises on rhetoric. In other words, they were to him a storehouse of facts. But they also filled him with emotions of pleasure. They charmed his ear by their cadences; they charmed his inner eye by their pictures; they charmed his moral nature by the examples they offered him of sublime beauty and bravery and patriotism. In short, they were to him a storehouse of ideas; and this, in the eyes of his teacher, was doubtless their chief value. But nowadays we need not use poetry as a storehouse of facts, and we need to use literature for this purpose only so far as a good style helps in the presentation of facts, as for example in the case of history. With our long list of sciences, natural and linguistic and moral, we are in no danger of ignoring the world of facts, and are therefore free to use literature, especially poetry, in order to appeal to the emotions of youth. Hence, in inquiring how we may best teach literature, we are really inquiring how we may best teach the literature of the imagination, — that is, poetry in a wide sense; for it would seem that literature used as a storehouse of facts might be taught like any other subject in the domain of fact.

But some one may ask, While all this is true enough, what has it to do with the practical teaching of literature? I answer that it has everything to do with it. If the chief reason for teaching literature be the fact that we shall thereby best appeal to the emotions, what is one to say of the amount of time given to the study of the history of literature, and to those critical, philological, and historical annotations that fill most of our literary textbooks? The history of literature is important enough, but it belongs to the domain of fact; it does not appeal primarily to the emotions. It is well for a child to know the names of great books and their authors; it is just as well that he should not say that Fielding wrote Tom Jones's Cabin or that Telemachus was a great French preacher of the seventeenth century, as I have known university students to do. But if the history of literature really appealed to the emotions, if it vitally affected any pupil, would he make such mistakes? The history of literature belongs to the domain of fact just as much as geography does, and the ability on the part of a child to reel off the names of authors and their dates is just as useless as his ability to tell the capital of Bolivia or to draw a map of Afghanistan. A certain amount of information about books and writers is useful, — the amount given in Mr. Stopford Brooke's and Professor Richardson's primers and in Mr. Brander Matthews's volume on American literature, — but not a bit more; for as intellectual training the history of literature is not nearly so efficient as many another study.

But if teaching the history of literature be beside the mark, if we wish to reach the emotions, what are we to say of criticism? I cannot see that we can say anything different. That pupil of mine who called Cowper's lines on the receipt of his mother's picture out of Norfolk an " ode " made an absurd mistake, but I am not at all sure that he would have been essentially better or happier if he had not made it. Critical appreciation is certainly better than uncritical, but, after all, appreciation is the main thing, and must precede criticism. Just how much critical, philological, and historical elucidation is needed to make a poem intelligible — for of course it has to be apprehended intellectually before it can produce its full emotional effect — is a hard matter to decide, but I am sure that the amount varies with the ages of the pupils. The younger the pupils, the simpler and less numerous the teacher's comments should be; for he has no right to be dealing with an obscure poem, and he must remember that he is not, or should not be, trying to teach his pupils facts. I am forced to conclude, then, that the common practice of putting into the hands of pupils a certain number of fully annotated classics, with the understanding that the unfortunate pupils are to be examined on the numerous facts contained in the notes and introductions, whatever may be claimed for it by college associations or by the editors of such books, is not the very best way of using literature as an appeal to the emotions of the young. Criticism, philology, and history are admirable handmaids to literature, but they are not literature, and they will not help us much in an appeal to the emotions. To make this appeal we must bring pupils in contact with the body of literature, and here is the crucial point of the problem before us.

But is not this to play into the hands of men like the late Professor Freeman, who opposed the establishment of a Chair of Literature at Oxford on the plea that we cannot examine on tastes and sympathies? If we are to make a minimum use of criticism, philology, and history, what manner of examination shall we be able to set our classes in literature? To this question Mr. Churton Collins replied that we ought to examine on Aristotle, Longinus, Quintilian, and Lessing; that is to say, on criticism. A very good answer so far as university students are concerned. The history and theory of literary composition, especially of poetry, should be included in every well-organized curriculum, and any competent teacher can examine on them. But though these studies may chasten the emotions, they do not primarily appeal to or awaken them, and for the purposes of the elementary teacher they are almost useless. Are such teachers, then, to be debarred from making use of those departments of literary study that admit of being tested by examination? I answer, Yes, so far as their main work is concerned. A small amount of literary history may be required and pupils may be examined on it, and perhaps a tiny amount of criticism, but for the most part school classes in literature should go scot-free from examination.

This will seem a hard saying to teachers enamored of school machinery, — who teach by cut-and-dried methods, and regard the school-day as a clock face, with the recitation hours corresponding to the figures, and themselves and their pupils to the hands. But the literary spirit and the mechanical spirit have long been sworn enemies, for machinery has no emotions; so, for the purposes of this paper, we need hardly consider the mechanical teacher, who had best keep his hands off literature. The born teacher, the teacher with a soul, — and I am optimist enough to believe that many of the men and women in this country who are wearing their lives away in the cause of education belong to this category, — will be glad to believe that there is at least one important study that need not and should not be pursued mechanically. The trouble will be not so much with the pupils and teachers as with the parents and statisticians, who want marks and grades, and that sort of partly necessary, partly hopeless thing. Now I have not the slightest idea how a child can be graded or marked on his emotions, yet I am sure that all teaching of literature that is worthy the name takes account of these chiefly. If this be true, should we not be brave enough to let the machinery go, and confine ourselves to the one pertinent and eternal question, How young souls can be best brought in contact with the spirit of literature?

If I may judge from my experience with college work, covering several years, and from my briefer experience with school work, I am forced to the conclusion that sympathetic reading on the part of the teacher should be the main method of presenting literature, especially poetry, to young minds. I have never got good results from the history of literature or from criticism except in the case of matured students, and I never expect to. I have examined hundreds of papers in the endeavor to find out what facts or ideas connected with literature appeal most to the young, and I have found that in eight out of ten cases it is the trivial or the bizarre. I remember a curious instance in point. I had been using Gosse's History of Eighteenth Century Literature, and I asked my class to give a brief account of the life of Alexander Pope. Judge of my astonishment when I found that three fourths of a large class had, without collusion, and no matter what the merits of the individual paper, copied verbatim the following sentence: " Pope, with features carved as if in ivory, and with the great melting eyes of an antelope, carried his brilliant head on a deformed and sickly body." Fortunately, in this case the trivial facts retained were rightly applied. In another case I was gravely informed that the poet Collins died "of a silk-bag shop," information that completely staggered me until I found that Mr. Gosse, innocent of any intention to mislead, had stated that Sterne died in "lodgings over a silk-bag shop." I need hardly cite further examples of utter and ridiculous confusion of names, for such examples are familiar to all teachers of experience. What I need to point out is that these mistakes are due, not to the stupidity of our pupils or to our own bad teaching, but to the fact that the history of literature is drier than mineralogy to any one who is not already fairly well read. Much the same thing may be said of criticism, only the chances of making mistakes are magnified through the elusive nature of the subject. It is well, certainly, to give a child some interesting information about great authors, and to try to teach him the distinctions between the broader categories of literature; but after this it seems to me that the primary and secondary teachers should rely mainly upon sympathetic reading. Certainly this is my experience with younger students. Whenever I find their attention flagging, I begin to read, and make my comments as brief as possible. In this way I have reached men who seemed at first sight to be hopeless. My most signal success was when I involuntarily set a baseball pitcher to committing certain sonnets of Shakspere to memory, while he was resting from practising new curves. I have always been proud of that achievement, but I believe it would be a by no means unusual one if teachers generally would criticise less and read more. The teacher must, of course, read sympathetically, or the result will be far from good. He must read with sincerity and enthusiasm and understanding, and with critical judgment. To try Browning's Red Cotton Night-Cap Country on a class of freshmen would be simply silly. To abstain from reading Byron to them on account of Mr. Saintsbury's recent utterances on the subject of his lordship's poetry would be equally silly. But there is, fortunately, a large amount of English and American poetry that is both noble and suitable to the comprehension of young minds. Where Emerson's Brahma will prove incomprehensible, his Concord Hymn will stir genuinely patriotic emotions.

It will be perceived that I am throwing a

great deal of responsibility on the teacher; and I think this is right, for the emotions of his pupils are like the strings of an instrument which he is to touch into life. After a while his intermediation will become less necessary, but at first it is essential in most cases. In spite of what many critics say, it is a fact that with a majority of children whatever literary appreciation they may have lies dormant until it is awakened by some skilful hand. It is better that this hand should be the teacher's, if only for the reason that the performance of such a service will add a pleasure to many a life wearied with the daily rounds of mechanical duty. I am sure that there is no teacher, man or woman, who would not be glad to have a half-hour set apart in each school-day in which arithmetics and grammars could be laid aside, and some favorite volume of poetry brought out from the desk and read with sympathy and enthusiasm. If I had a private school of my own, I should surely snatch the time for this, even if I had to have fewer maps drawn and fewer examples in partial payments worked. By the power of music Amphion built the walls of Thebes; by the power of poetic harmony we can try to build up the characters of our pupils. "What passion cannot music raise and quell?" asked Dryden, and we may ask the same question with regard to poetry. I have so much belief in the power of the "concord of sweet sounds" that I am inclined to say that many pupils will receive benefit from merely hearing great poetry read, even though it may not convey much meaning to their minds. Take, for example, this magnificent passage from Lycidas:

> "Ay me! whilst thee the shores and sounding seas
> Wash far away, where'er thy bones are hurled,
> Whether beyond the stormy Hebrides,
> Where thou perhaps under the whelming tide
> Visit'st the bottom of the monstrous world;
> Or whether thou, to our moist vows denied,
> Sleep'st by the fable of Bellerus old,
> Where the great vision of the guarded mount
> Looks toward Namancos and Bayona's hold;
> Look homeward, Angel, now, and melt with ruth,
> And, O ye dolphins, waft the hapless youth."

For the elucidation of these eleven lines I felt compelled to give recently nearly three pages of notes, over one page being concerned with the single word "Angel." Now I do not believe that the average schoolboy would have any clear notion as to who this Angel was, or as to what Bellerus or Namancos meant, but I think that the noble picture of the corpse of Lycidas washed by the sounding seas would appeal profoundly to his imagination, and that he would be the better for having heard his teacher read the lines. That he would be the better for nine out of ten of the critical and philological annotations that editors are constrained to make on the passage I see grave reason to doubt. The fact is that we have let the teacher of the Greek and Latin classics affect us by methods of minute analysis better fitted to the study of a dead than of a living language. These same classical teachers have, too, not a little to answer for, on account of the slight which time out of mind they have put on the purely literary side of their work. How many teachers of Latin, when reading Virgil, stop to comment on the sonorous quality of such a grand verse as

"Infandum, regina, jubes renovare dolorem,"

or upon this verse of Horace's,

"Cras ingens iterabimus æquor,"

which suggests comparison at once with Shakspere's "multitudinous seas," or with Matthew Arnold's

"The unplumb'd, salt, estranging sea"?

But the mention of Arnold reminds me that the stress I am laying on sympathetic reading of poetry by the teacher is merely an amplification of his advice that we should keep passages of great poetry in our minds, to serve as touchstones (perhaps tuning-forks would be a more accurate though less elegant metaphor) that will enable us to detect the presence or absence of truly poetic qualities in the verse we read. I should add also that this method of study is strictly in line with the best modern ideas; for pupils should be put in touch with a subject as a whole before they are set to studying its parts.

There are many other things that I should like to say, did space permit. I should like to protest against the use of great literature for exercises in parsing or for etymological or philological investigations; it ought even to be sparingly used for the purposes of reading-classes. I should like to protest against the lack of judgment shown by teachers and college professors in the texts they assign for study, — two books of Pope's Iliad, for example, in place of his Rape of the Lock, — a matter, however, in which we teachers of English are so far ahead of our friends who teach French and German that perhaps I ought to be thankful for the progress we have made. I should like finally to insist upon what I believe will some day be gen-

erally recognized, — the supremacy of literature as a study over all others that now
occupy the world's attention.   For when
everything is said, it is literature, and especially poetry, that has the first and the un-
disputed right to enter the audience-chamber
of the human soul.   Painting, sculpture,
music, the whole noble list of the sciences,
the lower but still important useful arts, may
and must continue to appeal and minister to
the spirit of man; but artistic prose and
poetry are the servants, — nay, are they not
rather the masters? — on which that spirit
has relied from the beginning of time, and
on which it will rely till time itself shall
end.

MR. HOWELLS AND ROMANTICISM

VIII

MR. HOWELLS AND ROMAN-
TICISM

MR. WILLIAM DEAN HOWELLS recently had occasion to speak a good word for the fiction that is being produced in our Southern States, but he prefaced his remarks by some uncomplimentary references to romantic fiction and to the Southern novelists, like Simms, Kennedy, and Esten Cooke, that wrote it. His exact words were: "I know that there were before the war novelists in South Carolina, in Maryland, and in Virginia deeply imbued with what our poor Spanish friends call the Walter-Scottismo, not to say the Fenimore-Cooperismo, of an outdated fashion of the world's fiction. But I have never read one of their books, and I should be able to say what they were like only at second hand."

It was extremely proper for Mr. Howells to refrain from discussing Simms, Kennedy, and Cooke, since he confessedly knows nothing about them, but was it proper for him to refer to them in quite the tone he used? Mr. Howells is too true a man to be arrogant, but sometimes his criticism is so aggressively modern that it falls little short of arrogance. There is surely no need of speaking of the fiction of sixty years ago as one would of a worn-out coat. It may be old-fashioned, but literary as well as other fashions are known to revive, and the material of a novel, which is human nature, does not unravel or become moth-eaten as the material of a coat does. Besides, no one wears an old coat who is not obliged to, while thousands of quite intelligent people still enjoy and read the romances their fathers read, and a whole school of writers has arisen whose aim is to break away from the realistic fiction Mr. Howells writes and advocates.

I am not at all disposed to blame Mr. Howells for praising the fiction he likes; all I claim is that it is uncatholic in him not to have a good word to say for writers who endeavored to do for their day what he is doing so well for his. His canon of criticism seems to be that what pleases the present is all a man need consider; quite as sure, if not a surer canon would be that there is some good in whatever has thoroughly pleased the bygone generations of men. Then, again, if there is any truth in the theory of evolution, the fiction of to-day must have been evolved out of the fiction of yesterday; hence the latter can hardly be foolish if the former be good, and present-day writers ought at least to cultivate the virtue of gratitude.

But is there any reason why a person who can enjoy as I have just done Mr. Howells's delightful Story of a Play should not be able to read with pleasure, as I did long since Simms's Eutaw, Kennedy's Horse-Shoe Robinson and Cooke's Virginia Comedians? Perhaps there is one rather effective reason, the fact that many people have an imperfect sympathy with the past. This is one of the chief reasons why such a poem as Paradise Lost is so little read to-day; but would it not be foolish to argue that great poem's worthlessness from its paucity of readers? Mr. Howells, of course, does not argue at all about the worthlessness of *ante bellum* Southern fiction, but the way in which he passes it over suggests that if he did argue, his argument would be based upon the inapplicability of that fiction to present conditions —which is tantamount to ignoring the fact that it is possible to get a great deal of pleasure out of any good artistic product of the past if we can put ourselves in touch with it. But that thousands of people can do this is a matter of every-day experience, hence it would be more becoming in the friends of realism to acknowledge with Horatio — for that gentleman was doubtless wise enough to agree with Hamlet — that there are more things than are dreamed of in their philosophy. There are some good things, however, in Mr. Howells's philosophy, and I shall now try to show what these are.

When Mr. Howells, consciously or unconsciously, endeavors to divert readers from the older romances, he shows himself, I think, to be an uncatholic critic; but in so far as his remarks affect latter-day writers, they seem to me to be altogether admirable. There can be no question that the art of fiction has developed; there is equally no question that those who write it to-day ought to be abreast of the art they practise. The realistic work of Balzac, Flaubert, Daudet, Zola, Tolstoi, Hardy and Howells has made it impossible for readers, not in fair sympathy with the past, to tolerate much of the crude work of sixty years ago. This is as it should be, and if the art of fiction develop, the writers of realistic fiction who are the masters to-day will be left behind in their turn, except in the case of such comprehensive geniuses as Balzac.

But if this be true, are not writers wasting their time, if, in revolt against present methods, they throw themselves back upon past methods without having profited from the teachings of contemporary masters? They may gain readers, of course, and if they have no other end in view their revolt is justified; but if they are conscientious artists, are they not making a mistake? For example, what permanent place in literature can the increasing swarm of men and women who are imitating Mr. Stanley Weyman expect to have? They have profited a little in point of style from the later masters, their knowledge of history and archæology is greater than that of the romancers of two generations ago, but they surely do not in most cases succeed in keeping their books from being mere *tours de force*. Almost every day a new historical romance comes to my table — now the scene is laid in the Italy of the fourteenth century, now in the France of the thirteenth; now it is in Wales, now in the Faroë Islands. Nearly always the story is told by the chief actor, who has hairbreadth escapes in plenty — in which neither author nor reader ought normally to take much interest, for they seem to be utterly factitious. How much more good these authors would be doing if they would only write as well as they could about the life around them.

The early romancers did not do this, to be sure, but they did do something their modern imitators cannot do — they breathed the spirit of romance, which was in the air of their times, into their souls and practically lived by it. The romantic thus became almost the real to them, and hence their works represented them truly. But there is no genuine spirit of romanticism abroad to-day; life was never more real and strenuous and earnest; hence our latter-day romancers do not give out what they breathe in. Their romanticism is artificial, factitious; it is the product of a literary fad which is itself the product of a premature literary revolt. Certainly realism when it passed into naturalism went too far and a revolt was needed; but it seems a pity that the revolters should not have gone back to sound realism and made a new departure from it. Men who have lost their way try to strike their path again at the point of divergence; they do not make for a deserted camp and pursue a backward trail therefrom. But this is just what our recent romancers have been doing, and if in any way Mr. Howells's criticisms can show them the folly of their course I trust that every word he writes will be seriously pondered. What I have just been saying will receive considerable illustration from a cursory examination of one of the most delightful books of Daudet — his autobiographic romance, Le Petit Chose (Little What 's-His-Name). The first part of this story is realistic in the best sense of the term; that is, it sticks close to the facts of experience while treating them in an idealistic way. Mere realism, not shot through with idealism, soon degenerates into naturalism, and is as unpleasant as an entirely unideal character is in real life. It was always impossible for Daudet to write without idealizing, but in the first part of Le Petit Chose his ideal picture of his boyhood was a true picture, which lost nothing by being pure at the same time.

In the second part of his story, however, while not ceasing to be idealistic, he did cease to be realistic and became romantic in a high degree. He left the facts of experience behind, with the result that his story lost both force and charm. He failed to give a picture of Bohemian Paris that would at all compare with those of Balzac or even with those which he himself gave later. He weakened his leading character and made the others either pathetic or commonplace. And all this resulted from the fact that when he ceased to rely upon his personal experiences, his feet ceased to rest upon the solid ground, and he began flitting like a pretty butterfly. If he had written a generation earlier, we should not have felt the weakness, for his story would have been all of a piece, and would have represented the best he had to give. Writing in 1868, however, he failed to profit by the example set by Balzac, and it was some time before he realized his mistake.

This book of Daudet's, then, illustrates admirably the fact that in an unromantic age it is useless to attempt to depart from the canons of true realism. These canons demanded that Daudet should keep his eye on both real and ideal life, and that he should not write merely a pretty and pathetic story ending in a happy marriage literally forced upon a ne'er-do-well by the singularly imprudent father of a much forgiving damsel. Later in his life, Daudet, having learned the value of true realism, regretted that he had written Le Petit Chose, for he felt that he could have turned his youthful experiences to better account. Perhaps he was wrong in this; at least, it is certain that the first half, in which he did not aim at romantic effects, is one of the most perfect descriptions of the checkered experience of a child and youth that can be found in literature. And it has these merits because it is true to facts rather than to mere desires. The romancer consults desires, and so builds air castles in which the active men and women of to-day do not care to tarry. The naturalist, forgetting the ideal, is only too likely to construct sties in which no clean-minded person will feel comfortable for a moment. The true realist builds a solid and substantial house in which the intelligent reader delights to linger. Thus we perceive that when Mr. Howells praises realism he is doing all writers of fiction a service, although we need not, as readers, agree with his slighting remarks with regard to the romances that delighted our grandfathers.

IX

TENNYSON AND MUSSET ONCE MORE

IX

TENNYSON AND MUSSET
ONCE MORE.

I HAD just ceased reading, a few weeks since, the interesting but rather bulky volumes which the present Lord Tennyson has devoted to the memory of his distinguished father, when chance led me to examine in succession two yellow-backed books published this year in Paris (1897). They were M. Paul Mariéton's Une Histoire d'Amour and the letters of George Sand to Alfred de Musset and to Ste. Beuve, with an introduction by M. S. Rocheblave. No contrast could have been greater than that afforded by the severe restraint of the Tennyson memoir and the utter *abandon* of the two latest contributions to the history of the most famous love affair of the nineteenth century. The impulse to draw a sort of Plutarchian parallel was almost irresistible, and equally potent was the desire to read once more Taine's well-known comparison of Tennyson and Musset in the last chapter of his Histoire de la Littérature Anglaise.

We all remember how Taine contrasted the two poets and the respective publics for which they wrote, and we recall the impressionist note with which he closed what he tried to make a rigidly scientific work — "but I prefer Alfred de Musset." We can most of us probably, if we were under Tennyson's influence when we read these words — and who of us was not in those golden days? — remember the fine scorn we felt for the Frenchman who had the audacity to maintain that his country, land of broken-backed Alexandrines as it was, had produced a poet worthy of being mentioned in the same breath with the author of Œnone, Maud, and Elaine. This fine scorn which we felt then has lingered on with some people, and actually intrudes itself into the appendix to the second volume of the Tennyson memoir, where the late Professor Palgrave permitted himself to speak of M. Taine as a "lively critic." But to those of us who have been allowed to see the error of our way through our reading of Hugo, Leconte de Lisle, and Musset himself, who have learned to our surprise that much of what our teachers had told us about the insufficiency of the French language to the expression of high poetic thought and sentiment was due to mere ignorance on their part, a doubt has perhaps come more than once whether Taine was not partly justified in his preference for Musset over Tennyson — a doubt which the perusal of the four volumes named above does not altogether allay. For from contrasting the lives of the two poets, one proceeds inevitably to the weighing and contrasting of their works.

With regard to the memoir of Tennyson little need be said. Since its appearance in October last there has been no such personage as an "indolent reviewer" to be found in the land. The critics seem to have gone down like ninepins before it, and they are still lying in a state of prostrate and hardly becoming adulation. Could the Laureate have foreseen their postures, he would probably have burned more letters than he did, and would have been still more determined to have his poem, The Gleam, received as the sole authorized memorial of his life. The gift of prescience was not his, however, and so we are left to wonder whether the reading world of a hundred years from now will really peruse with rapture the letters of Queen Victoria, the reminiscences of Mr. Tyndall and

other famous contemporaries, the mere social
notes of Mr. Lowell and his peers, the extracts from private diaries, that make up a
large portion of these volumes which the
critics have already placed by the side of
Boswell's Johnson. But whatever our conclusions as to the mortality or immortality of
this memoir in its present bulky shape, we
should surely be blind if we failed to recognize the essential nobility of the life portrayed. The man whom the English have
been extolling, while their French neighbors
have been picking his great rival to pieces,
was obviously a noble and conscientious
artist in verse, a poet fully impressed with
the sacred nature of his calling, a critic of
remarkably acute powers, a widely read and
observant student of nature and of men, an
intensely spiritual seeker after God, a loyal
patriot and friend — in short, an ideal character of a high and attractive type,

Such was the man — except perhaps in his
rôle of critic — that had stood out behind the
Poems; such is the man that stands out behind the Biography. But neither the poetry
nor the memoir proves Tennyson to have
been the profound seer that Mr. Gladstone
and other contemporaries thought him, nor
does either source of information disprove

the charge that he was morbidly sensitive, and hence unable to give full expression to the lyric passion that was a fundamental constituent of his nature. It is in view of this charge that the destruction of the letters to Arthur Hallam and to Miss Sellwood before she became Lady Tennyson is so much to be regretted. Whatever the admirers of Maud may say, the Tennyson that we know through his poems after 1842 and through the memoir is rather the poet of idyll, elegy, and artificial epic than the poet of lyrical passion, whether of love or grief. That he was profoundly passionate we have reason to believe from the evidence of friends, from some of the early poems — perhaps FitzGerald's well-known inability to appreciate fully the later poems came from his missing the adequate expression of this passion, and not from the fact, ungenerously urged by the present Lord Tennyson, that he did not see the faulted verses in manuscript — and from lyric outbursts in the long roll of poems that succeeded the volumes of 1842. But, whatever the cause, the atmosphere about the matured poet did not furnish sufficient oxygen for the flame of his passion, and it flickered and burned low. Yet it was diverted rather than suppressed, and it kindled his other poetic powers. He became the artist passionate for perfection, he searched the ages for noble characters, and imparted some passion to them, his spirituality and his patriotism glowed brighter with the years, even the pessimistic utterances of his latter days had a certain lurid quality about them. So at least it seems to some of us, and prizing though we do what he has chosen to give us, we miss both in the poetry and in the life that lyrical expression of Tennyson's innermost nature which he would surely have given us had he been a contemporary of Byron's or a countryman of Musset's. It is vain to tell us that he took the more dignified course, that he had a right to keep his deepest and most sacred emotions hidden from the world; it is vain to quote to us from Leconte de Lisle's fine sonnet, Les Montreurs, which derives its interest from the very quality its author denounces in others. If Tennyson had not shown us that his real strength or a great part of his real strength lay in the lyrical expression of his passion, we should be content to praise him as we do reflective poets like Wordsworth; but having given us reason to believe that he had in him the fire that burned in Sappho and Catullus, in Shakspere, Byron, and Musset, he disappoints us by rarely or never breaking into flame, either in his verse or in the biography which his son has constructed according to his wishes. "From him that hath not, even that which he hath shall be taken away." Are we unreasonable in our demands upon Tennyson? Ought we to be contented with the noble work he has given us? Perhaps so; yet a few of us at least, after reading the memoir and going back to the poems, have found ourselves asking for precisely what Taine demanded over thirty years ago, and what he averred he found in Alfred de Musset. But this leads us naturally to take account of our two yellow French twelvemos, which show up so pitifully in appearance beside the royal English octavos.

It would not be true to say that the Parisian public has been for the past eighteen months as busy discussing the relations of Musset and George Sand as the English-speaking public has been for a shorter period with regard to the secluded life of the recluse of Farringford — for they have a multitude of things to talk about in Paris — but it is certainly true that the famous love-story has attracted a great deal of attention, and that Sandists and Mussetists have been waging a new Battle of the Books, or else floundering once more in that old Slough of Scandals which Bunyan forgot to describe for us. M. Mariéton's book, for example, might seem to be hurled at his Sandist adversaries from out the very midst of the slough, for while giving a history of the whole love-affair it devotes itself mainly to answering in the affirmative one question important to the controversy — viz., Was George Sand unfaithful to Musset *during* the latter's illness at Venice, or was she not? An affirmative answer to this unsavory question not only convicts George Sand of deliberate falsification, but also convicts her, author though she be, of La Mare au Diable, of being far looser in her actions than that Juliette of hers who went back to her scoundrel lover, Leone Leoni. M. Mariéton having made an affirmative answer based on various hitherto unedited documents, it is, of course, in order for a Sandist like M. Rocheblave to call the authenticity of the documents into question, although one could wish that he had better grounds for doing so than the mere fact that they are contradicted by certain statements of George Sand, a not uninterested party. Indeed, throughout this whole controversy a partisan lack of care in weighing evidence is as apparent as it is in literary controversies with which we are more familiar — for example, that which is continually being waged over the life of Shelley.

It would not be profitable to undertake a minute analysis either of M. Mariéton's book or of George Sand's passionate letters. The details of the affair may be left to those who care to go to the sources; its outlines are well known and may be easily recalled. We all remember that by the spring of 1833 Madame Dudevant had broken with Jules Sandeau, and was lying in the trough of the sea of romanticism waiting to be washed higher by its on-coming waves. With her inherited passions, with her artistic instincts, with her banal experience of married life, and with her stimulating contact with literary success and the romantic fervor of the times, she had no chance to escape a psychological crisis of the most acute kind. A similar fate was impending over Alfred de Musset. The normal debauchery of an idle, aristocratic youth about town, the easy success obtained with the Cénacle by his Andalusian verses, could not satisfy the most passionate heart in Europe now that Byron was dead. He, too, must have his psychological crisis, and it would be more acute than George Sand's. Whether Ste. Beuve perceived all this when he played the part of uncle to the modern

Cressida, and tried to bring the romantic pair together is not clear; but it is at least certain that from the time they first met, in June, 1833, the more inflammable heart was set aglow, and that the more indurated one speedily responded. Then, while Tennyson was in the flush of his grief for Arthur Hallam, came the seclusion of the *quai Malaquais*, the honeymoon — for such the infatuated lovers really deemed it — at Fontainebleau, so well described in the Confession and in Elle et Lui, then the fateful journey to Italy.

The land of lovers had known few more passionately sincere for the time being than these two, and it had known few fates more really tragic than that which awaited them. For their passions, raging outside the bounds of law, moral as well as physical, had to rise to the height like waves and then break. Musset's broke first. His nerves were strained from his recent life of dissipation, and his colossal *amour-propre* revolted from the self-centred independence of a companion who could write for hours without taking note of his presence. He ruptured the alliance by harsh words, and probably by acts which he lived to regret and despise. Then came the illness at Venice, the appearance of

Dr. Pietro Pagello upon the scene, the faithlessness of George Sand, the fantastic attempt of Musset to reconcile himself to a *ménage à trois*, and finally his departure for Paris a worn-out wreck of body, mind, and soul. Nemesis had attached herself to him, seeming to forget George Sand left behind in unromantic relations with Pagello. But Nemesis was not really forgetful. She presided over the letters, passionate on both sides, though with that curious maternal note on the woman's part that one finds never leaving her, which were sent over the Alps; she presided over the undignified return journey made by George Sand with Pagello in leash; she presided over the renewals of intimacy, the swift partings, the letters, the private journals, the tears and wailings of the remainder of that eventful year, 1834; and finally she has presided ever since over the literary exploitation of the whole frantic episode, over the quarrels raised by the publication of Elle et Lui and Lui et Elle, and the contentions of the Sandists and Mussetists of the present day.

I have no desire to incur her displeasure by going too deeply into these unpleasant matters myself, but there are at least two points, one specific and one general, that

ought to be touched on. The first is how far
M. Mariéton's anti-Sand position is tenable.
He has published a journal of Dr. Pagello
himself, an incriminating romantic fragment
by George Sand, entitled En Morée, by
means of which, it is claimed, she made her
love known to the physician, and a number
of interesting and valuable letters of Musset
chosen from the correspondence still somewhat jealously guarded by the poet's sister.
In addition he gives two drafts in Paul de
Musset's handwriting of the alleged account
dictated by Alfred of the now famous " vision "
of the sick-room at Venice and its consequences, which readers of Lui et Elle have
not forgotten. Judged impartially, these documents, if genuine, are the most damaging
testimony yet brought against George Sand's
character. As has been intimated, doubt is
thrown upon their authenticity by her friends,
but although M. Mariéton has not given us
all the information that could be desired
about them, it is hard to see how the journal
of Pagello (who was living at a great old age
when Mariéton wrote but has since died) can
be thrown out of court, and if that stays,
the fragment En Morée, George Sand's *gage
d'amour*, stays also. Indeed, there are *à priori* reasons why it should stay, for Pagello

could read French fluently, but spoke it poorly, while George Sand was just picking up Italian. A few romantic pages in her facile style would, therefore, be the most natural and effectual means she could choose for a confession of so delicate a nature.

As for M. Mariéton's reliance upon the truth of Paul de Musset's sick-room scene, it is only in keeping with his confidence in the latter's entire defence of his brother. M. Mariéton, relying, it would seem, upon Madame Lardin de Musset, and ignoring the general verdict with regard to Paul's character, declares that the latter's novel *sweats truth (sue la vérité)* where we should prefer to say that it perspires dulness. In this frank credence in Paul de Musset he is certainly bold, but if the dictated memoranda can be shown by examination of watermarks, etc., to bear the date assigned them, December, 1852, nearly four years and a half before Alfred de Musset's death, they are certainly documents that cannot be lightly treated. They are supported, too, by a small piece of corroborative evidence that has not, perhaps, been sufficiently noticed. Alfred de Musset's Confession d'un Enfant du Siècle, in which he chivalrously takes all the blame on himself and absolves George Sand, is frequently quoted as an authority for the fidelity of its description of the Fontaynebleau expedition — for example, by Madame Arvède Barine in her interesting sketch of Musset — but is not generally relied on as an authority for Paul de Musset's version of the sick-room incident. Yet the single tea-cup drunk out of by the two lovers (George Sand and Pagello), which figures in Lui et Elle, figures also in the Confession. Was it one of the touches that made George Sand weep when she read Alfred's novel? And what have the Sandists done with this incriminating tea-cup? The answer comes naturally enough — they have swallowed it; or else, speaking seriously, we may suppose that they infer that Paul de Musset borrowed the tea-cup scene from Alfred, and then embellished it in his own peculiarly exasperating manner.

The second point that must be touched on is the question what possible value can attach to books treating of such an unpleasant episode. Nearly all the reviewers have expatiated on the delight they experienced when they found the Tennyson volumes free from scandal, so that one is left to infer that unless they were indulging in cant, British and American critics are above all vulgar curiosity, and would prefer to draw a veil over the inner history of literary men, except when, as in Tennyson's case, there is practically nothing to hide. It is needless to say that such is not the French view, and that no one who has studied his Ste. Beuve will continue to throw his influence on the side of British cant. We shall do well to wish that our literary heroes and heroines would lead clean lives, but if they will not, and we propose to be their critics, we must follow them at least to the banks of the Slough of Scandals. From this point of view, then, the books we are considering should have been published, and should be read by all serious students of George Sand and of Alfred de Musset. That they will be read by many who are not serious students is, of course, matter for regret; but so is religious hypocrisy, and surely no one would suggest that we should do away with all religions in order to put an end to the propagation of Tartuffes.

But the documents contained in these books have claims to be regarded as something far higher than mere evidence in a famous case of scandal. The letters that passed between the two lovers are among the most intense ever written, and are not merely precious sources of information for all students of Romanticism, but also lyrical out-bursts of two passionate hearts that must be ranked in the future but little below the in-comparable Nuits of the more poetical and sorely strained of the two protagonists of this drama of suffering. Here, indeed, we find the best excuse for the publication of all the volumes and essays that have dealt with this remarkable episode. Out of them some anthologist, perhaps, still unborn, will be able to cull a volume of letters, poems, pages of description and extracts from private journals that will be a source of delight to all who care for the literature of passion, and will serve to make the memory of Musset and George Sand, as the former predicted, as abiding as that of Abélard and Héloïse. With the lapse of years the grosser features of the story will be more or less eliminated, and the flame of passion, which in Musset's case at least was never really extinguished, will burn clearly for all time. It is, of course, impossible to prove such statements as these, for the charge of romantic extravagance and insin-cerity may be brought against the lovers, and such a charge can never be thoroughly refuted. Documents relative to any great passion will always be judged favorably or unfavorably, according to the capacity of the critic or reader to understand or experience passion. Shakspere's Sonnets have caused some people to wonder why he wrote them, and have been held by other people not to refer to any specific passions at all. Still one may at least cite a few burning passages from these letters that will help to indicate the perfervid character of the whole correspondence.

Here is how Musset, on April 30th, 1834, could write to the woman who had abandoned him:

" O mon enfant chérie, lorsque tu m'aimais, m'as-tu jamais trompé? Quel reproche ai-je jamais eu à te faire pendant sept mois que je t'ai vue, jour par jour? Et quel est donc le lâche misérable qui appelle perfide la femme qui l'estime assez pour l'avertir que son heure est venue? Le mensonge, voilà ce que j'abhorre, ce qui me rend le plus défiant des hommes, peut-être le plus malheureux. Mais tu es aussi sincère que tu es noble et orgueilleuse."

Again he writes later in the year, after relations have been renewed, only to bring anguish to both, and when he feels that they must have one final interview and part:

" Que ce ne soit pas l'adieu de monsieur Un tel et de madame Une telle. Que ce soient deux âmes qui ont souffert, deux intelligences souffrantes, deux aigles blessés qui se rencontrent dans le ciel, et qui échangent un cri de douleur avant de se séparer pour l'éternité."

Was not the man who could write thus justified in writing later:

"La postérité répétera nos noms comme ceux de ces amants immortels qui n'en ont plus qu'un à eux deux, comme Roméo et Juliette, comme Héloïse et Abélard."

One citation from George Sand's equally moving letters must suffice. Let us take it from the highly wrought epistle of June 15th, 1834:

"Vois combien tu te trompais quand tu te croyais usé par les plaisirs et abruti par l'expérience! Vois que ton corps s'est renouvelé et que ton âme sort de sa chrysalide. Si, dans son engourdissement, elle a produit de si beaux poèmes, quels sentiments, quelles idées en sortiront maintenant qu'elle a déployé ses ailes. Aime et écris, c'est ta vocation, mon ami. Monte vers Dieu sur les rayons de ton génie et envoie ta muse sur la terre raconter aux hommes les mystères de l'amour et de la foi."

Alfred de Musset took his "brother George" at her word, and the next two years were the most fruitful of his life. But how

does the work produced under such circumstances, together with that of his youth and
of his sterile later years, compare with that
of his more fortunate British contemporary —
for to compare the lives of the two men further
is surely unnecessary? Putting to one side
the delightful comedies and *contes*, have we
any right to share Taine's preference for
Musset's poetry as compared with that of
Tennyson? Obviously not, if Tennyson's
admirers, like Mr. Aldrich and Dr. Van Dyke,
are justified in maintaining that their favorite
must rank next to Shakspere and Milton in
the hierarchy of the English poets. If the
Idylls of the King be a sustained and noble
epic rather than the " boudoir epic " Mr.
Frederic Harrison finds them to be; if In
Memoriam be really the most profound poem
of the century rather than an unequal series of
elegiac verses appealing to an over-emotional
and not very thoughtful public ; if Maud fails
in any way to suggest a sensational novel, and
The Princess is a work of perfect, not hybrid
art, then these poems, together with the
ballads, the idylls of English life, the mono-
logues, and the wonderful songs, are clearly
enough to set Tennyson far above the
author of the Nuits, the Letter to Lamartine,
and the Stanzas to Malibran. If, however,

Tennyson's longer poems are to be forgotten save for selected passages, and if his reputation is to rest on the shorter poems in his early manner and on the tradition of his artistic command of rhythm and diction; if, furthermore, the world that is now sated with composite art renews its youth through some stirring crisis, and once more demands passion as a primary element of literature, will the bard of Aldworth and Farringford hold his own against the poet of the streets of Paris? Perhaps he may, in spite of all that may be said about the suppression of his passion and about the deficiencies of his longer poems. Should the world come once more to demand passion, it will probably be Byron that will eclipse Tennyson, not Alfred de Musset, whose star will nevertheless rise splendidly in the poetic heavens. For, after all, Musset's strictly poetical work, great as it is at its best, is not, it would seem, sufficient in amount to balance that of Tennyson, even if the latter poet is shorn of half his present glory by envious time. But leaving the question of the relative position of the two poets aside, it is certainly permissible for those who care for the lyrical expression of intense passion to maintain that they find little or nothing in Tennyson that takes the place for them of

Musset's chief poems.   If they are pressed to point out a passage illustrating the kind of passion they demand from Tennyson, but do not find, they may quote these lines from the Nuit de Mai:

> " J'ai vu le temps où ma jeunesse
> Sur mes lèvres était sans cesse
> Prête à chanter comme un oiseau ;
> Mais j'ai souffert un dur martyre,
> Et le moins que j'en pourrais dire,
> Si je l'essayais sur ma lyre,
> *La briserait comme un roseau.*"

" Here," they may say, " is the ' lyric cry ' which we have missed more or less in British poetry since the days of Byron," and if they are pressed to describe still further the voice that has moved them so profoundly, they may reply, quoting the Stanzas to Malibran:

> " C'est cette voix du cœur qui seule au cœur arrive,
> Que nul autre, après toi, ne nous rendra jamais."